Praise for On the Edge of Grace

"The novel's pacing is steady, with moments of tension and introspection balanced by lighter, heartwarming scenes, and Jones's background as a marriage and family therapist is evident in her nuanced portrayal of relationships and their emotional complexities. She infuses the narrative with faith-based reflections, adding depth to the themes of forgiveness and grace, as Blou tries to decide whether she and Gable can weather the storm and reunite, or if she needs to start over and build something from the ground up with someone else. This is a compelling debut that offers heartfelt explorations of life's messiness and the quiet strength it takes to rebuild. Fans of character-driven stories with themes of redemption and emotional healing will find it deeply satisfying."

—Publishers Weekly

ON THE EDGE OF GRACE

OF GRACE

A Novel

April Y. Jones

Library of Congress Control Number: 2025918123

IBSN 978-1-7370485-8-9 (Paperback)

Author's Note

Hi, Friends,

Thank you so much for taking an interest in reading my book. It means the world to me, and I truly hope you find the same joy in reading it that I found in writing it.

Before you begin, I want to offer a gentle note of consideration. While this is a work of fiction, some of the characters face challenges that may be emotionally difficult for some readers. The story includes references to death during childbirth, cancer, and a fictional rare illness with a fictional treatment.

If you choose to continue, please do so with care and kindness toward your own heart. Your well-being matters deeply to me.

With gratitude,

April

To Boss-

What is meant to be will be.
This one is for you,
Mr. Love of My Life

Chapter One

As I sat in the living room of our recently purchased, sixty-two-hundred-square-foot home, I could barely finish reading the letter written and left by my husband through the tears that blurred my vision. I had read the letter five times within the last hour, trying to make sense of it. I'd found the letter right after I got home from working for ten hours—four hours in court and six hours in the office. After the first time I'd read it, I thought, *This must be a joke.* His empty closet confirmed, it was not. My heart felt as if it was sinking deeper into my chest as I read the letter now for the sixth time.

Blou, I am so sorry to do this, but I'm doing this for you because I love you with all my heart.

That was the sentence in this nightmare of a letter that struck a nerve as I read it again.

How was my husband, whom I've been happily married to for almost seven years, leaving me…for me? How did someone who claimed to love me with all his heart think a sick and twisted plan to suddenly abandon me was a good idea? No warning, no heart-to-heart conversation, just pack up and leave with very few answers. I just couldn't wrap my head around his logic.

Sweet Blou, you are the love of my life. I do not want a divorce. I am sick, and I just need some time to figure things out before I can come back to you—if I am ever well enough to come back to you. Only time will tell, and I need that time.

"This man must think I'm Boo-Boo the Fool," my sharp voice rang out in disbelief mingled with anger. Gable couldn't possibly think that I was going to fall for such a lame excuse. If he was sick—really sick— why wouldn't he just talk to me? And what kind of sickness did he have, exactly? The letter was nebulous, lacking any detail about the illness he was claiming. Just a string of sentiments wrapped in uncertainty with a vague explanation, as if that was supposed to make it better—sweet nothings.

Since I'd found this letter sitting on the coffee table addressed to, *Blou, the One True Love of My Life,* I had cycled through a storm of emotions. I'd felt denial, shock, and sadness among other feelings I couldn't even name, but now anger danced in the forefront, demanding my attention. I had called his phone at least twenty-five times—each call met with his cheery voicemail. Each time I heard his voice, my heart sank a little more, my head pounded a little harder, and the urge to wring his neck intensified.

I never claimed to have had a perfect life or an unflawed marriage, but things had been amazing between Gable and me—at least I thought they were. We had our share of disagreements, but they were nothing more than the average marital quarrels. We made a point to still date regularly. Sex had slowed down just a little over the past few years, but it was still often and enjoyable. I couldn't think of one reason that would be good enough for him to walk away from everything we'd built together.

The personalized ring tone assigned specifically for my best friend interrupted my thoughts and dragged me out of rumination over this letter. I picked up the phone and hesitated to tap the green phone icon displayed on the screen to answer. I set the phone back down and let it ring. If I sent the call to voicemail, she would just call right back. I didn't want to talk. If I answered, she would know something was wrong. She'd hear it in my voice, and if I had to explain this mind-blowing, gut-wrenching letter to anyone right now, more than likely sobs and wails would come pouring out instead of audible words.

The phone lit up and rang again, blaring the same ring tone, indicating that my best friend was calling again. I resolved that she wouldn't stop calling until I answered, so begrudgingly, I did.

"Neveah, girl, what's up?" I managed to get out as a bubble rose up from my gut and into my throat.

"Blou! Girl, hey. I have some awesome news." Neveah's bubbly energy normally rubbed off on me, regardless of what mood I was in at the time. She was almost always cheerful and lively. I loved that about her because her felicitous vibe was one that seemed to put me at ease. Normally, I would smile just hearing the excitement in her voice and anxiously await whatever the great news was so I could also share in her joy. But now, at this moment, I couldn't muster up even a mustard seed of joy.

I assumed she was going to tell me her wonderful news about the next big account she had closed. I was always the first person she called to tell when she knocked out a goal at work. I knew she had been working on closing an account that could open the door for her to become a partner at the marketing consulting firm she'd been pouring her heart and sweat into. This must be what this was about.

I opened my mouth to offer my usual "What's good, sis" with equal excitement like I did any other time, but all I could do was release a visceral moan right before I lost complete control of my emotions and began to sob uncontrollably.

"Blou Rivers-Whitmore, girl, what is happening right now? You know what, I'm on my way over right now."

"No." I managed to push through the sobbing.

"Girl, bye. I'll be right there." Neveah hung up.

I let out a long sigh, put my phone on Do Not Disturb before anyone else called and went into the kitchen to grab a bottle of wine and two wine glasses. As much as I wanted to be alone right now, I might as well embrace the idea of company because if I didn't open the door, Neveah would just use the spare key hidden under the large terracotta on my front porch to let herself in.

I set the wine and glasses on the coffee table in the gathering room and decided to wash up. The least I could do was wipe the running mascara from my face and change out of the clothes I'd worn to court before my best friend arrived. If nothing else happened good today, at least the client I represented won everything she wanted in her divorce settlement.

I stepped into the spacious custom closet that was a spare bedroom just two weeks ago. When Gable suggested that I use this room to build my dream closet I didn't hesitate to hire contractors to make it happen. I know he was hoping that one of the other two spare rooms would soon be a nursery, but he also knew that I didn't want a child—or rather, I *couldn't* have a child. How could I put myself in the same devastating situation that took my mother's life when I was ten years old? The same could happen to me during my accouchement. So, no, I can't have a child. Not for myself, not for Gable, or any other man.

Gable suggested we adopt, but even when I thought of adopting, my stomach twisted into a tight knot, anxiety washed over me, and I could feel panic clenching my chest. What if we did adopt and ironically, I died and left a child motherless—like my mother died, leaving me behind. To make matters worse, my father died of cancer when I was just fifteen. And now look, Gable was claiming he was sick. What if we had adopted, if we did have a child…Just the thoughts made my stomach turn.

Suddenly, dizziness rushed over me and my stomach felt as though it was in a backflip competition with Simone Biles in the Olympics. I ran to the bathroom, thanking God I had chosen the in-law suite for my custom closet since it had its own ensuite bath room. I folded to my knees and grasped the toilet just in time for today's lunch to make its debut. I don't know what was making me sicker, that my marriage might be over and yet another person was leaving me or just the thought of having children and leaving them motherless and fatherless, in a world filled with so many people but still alone.

Once more, words from Gable's letter forced themselves into my thoughts:

I do wish that you would be patient with me, but it would be selfish to ask you to wait for me when I don't know what will happen as I seek treatment. If the wait becomes too much of a burden for you, you have my blessing to move on.

Fresh tears stung my eyes. I shook my mind free from those words because I didn't think I had the capacity to process them right now.

Slowly lifting myself from the floor with the support of the toilet, I flushed and watched as my nerves cleared the bowl. At the sink, I rinsed my mouth, brushed my teeth, and washed my face. As I was about to walk away, I caught a glimpse of my worn-out face in the mirror. The sudden stress of that letter seemed to have aged my naturally younger looking face a few years just within minutes. I turned back and stared directly into the face of the woman looking back at me. Melancholy and dejection emitted sadness from her red, puffy eyes. "Why is this happening to me again? Why does everyone leave me?"

My voice cracked as I whispered to my reflection in the mirror. In the blink of an eye, the reflection that had just been a thirty-one-year-old woman was now my ten-year-old self staring back, meeting my eyes with warmth laced with concern and an unspoken sorrow. A beautiful little girl with a smooth mocha complexion and a bronze undertone. Her hair neatly tucked into a kinky afro puff, glistering from coconut oil and shea butter. Her expression mimicked mine as I attempted to smile at her with a smile that didn't quite reach my eyes.

I jumped, startled, as I heard Neveah calling my name from somewhere in the house. I rushed out of the bathroom as I peeled off the cream high-waisted dress pants and the blouse Gable had picked out that I'd purchased from Bloomingdale's during this past weekend's shopping spree. "Coming," I yelled, pulling open the drawer that held my loungewear. I took out a gray cashmere set and threw it on.

"So, let me get this straight: He left you because he found out he's sick with some rare disease that you had no clue he has. He decided to admit himself into a clinical trial that may or may not save his life. He doesn't want you around him during this process because of everything you've already been through with the death of your mom and then watching your dad die from cancer?"

Neveah handed the letter back to me, perplexed, as she summarized what Gable had written. I thought it would be much easier for her to read it for herself because speaking the words just made it seem even more unbelievable.

I sat quietly next to Neveah on the white lush couch she'd helped me pick out to pop perfectly with the navy, gray, and coral accents splashed throughout the gathering room also displayed in the wall paintings and whatnots that decorated the walls and shelves.

She gently grabbed my trembling hand. "Blou, what are you going to do?" Her voice was gentle. I looked at my friend. Empathy was sketched on her beautiful reddish-brown face. Her jet-black curly hair was pulled back into a ponytail. I noticed for the first time since she'd gotten here that she was wearing purple Actively Black spandex leggings that hugged her hourglass shape and a matching sports bra, which meant she must have been on the way to the gym. I could tell she hadn't worked out yet because I could smell her favorite body spray, which carried a fresh scent of vanilla and sugar with no hints that she had been sweating.

I opened my mouth to speak but was at a loss for words. Her question echoed in my mind. The tears that I had been fighting so hard to hold back slid down my cheeks. I looked away. With fear invading my space, I felt panic gripping my throat as my chest tightened. The tighter the squeeze, the more I struggled to catch the rapid breaths that escaped me.

"Hey," Neveah said softly, her hand still intertwined with mine.

"Let's slow down. You do not have to figure this all out right now, sweetie."

She pulled me into her. I laid my head on her shoulder. I could feel her smoothing my kinky curly afro as she did when we were teenagers sitting beside me at the hospital right after my father took his last breath. Her warm embrace always brought me comfort.

My breathing began to steady as I slowly breathed through my nose and out through my mouth, counting during both inhale and exhale. After the panic settled, I straightened my body from Neveah's embrace. She reached for the bottle of House of Brown red blend wine sitting on the coffee table and poured us both a generous serving. I gladly took the glass to my lips and took a big gulp.

"If I can just talk to him and make sense of all this, it might be easier to accept. He has to know that not talking to me is much harder on me. He said in his letter that it's easier for him to write to me than to speak to me over the phone and that he will be sending another letter soon. I know he won't disclose any details about his whereabouts because he thinks I'll show up."

Neveah raised her brows and tilted her head, giving me that you-better-believe-it, look. "Of course we will show up."

I shot back a knowing look. "On the first thing smoking." We bumped fists.

I let out a heavy sigh. "My brain is on overload, and I feel like a big dark hole sits in my chest where my heart used to be. I need something to distract me from the ache—at least for now. What was your good news?"

Neveah hesitated to answer. "Um. Well, that can wait. Let's focus on you."

"Neveah, I need the focus off me right now and off my mess of a life. I need to hear something good. Please, tell me."

Neveah closed her eyes. With her lips pursed together, she breathed in and then let out a long breath. "Lukas asked me to marry him."

My eyes widened. "No! Girl, what?!" With joy welling up inside of me, I was about to jump out of my seat when Neveah rested a hand on my leg.

"Uh-uh. Don't get too excited. I said I need to think about it."

"OK, girl. Then how is this good news again?"

"Girl, because now I know that I'm wifey material for somebody. Being in a four-year relationship with Derrick and he never asked me to marry him had me thinking I just might not be cut out for marriage, especially with the amount of time I put into my career. You know I had to go to therapy after that relationship ended. We argued all the time, and every time I was the one compromising or giving up something to appease him."

"Derrick had commitment issues and obviously some control issues too. And like I've told you before, I strongly believe he had a problem with you making more money than him, even though he's successful himself. It was not you. But Lukas, y'all have been together for two years, and he already knows what he wants. Girl, he loves you. He accepts you for who you are, and he is supportive of everything you do. What's the problem?"

"Well, for one, he has been married before and has two children with his ex-wife. He wants to get married next year, and once we get married, I'll become a mother to his children too—right now I'm just his girlfriend. I absolutely adore his children, but I have not met their mom. I'm not sure if I'm ready for the baby mama drama." Neveah rolled her eyes, and finger signed a quotation at the words, baby mama.

I giggled. I love Neveah but she could be so dramatic sometimes. "How do you know there will be any baby mama drama?" I repeated the same quotation motion with my fingers.

"You remember how crazy things were between my mom and my dad after they were divorced. I don't want to go through what my mom put my dad and his wife through when he got remarried. I would rather wait until his kids are grown."

"I hear you, sis, but maybe you should meet her before you assume she's a replica of your mother. I mean I love Mama Lucee, but she did create a lot of drama. You remember that time Ms. Nandi accompanied your dad to our eighth-grade graduation and your mom caused a scene in the parking lot after the ceremony because he brought her with him? Your mom was so loud. She said, 'This was supposed to be an accomplishment for her parents to share with her. Not with your little whore.'" I laughed.

"And the time when you told your mom that *Momma Didi* took you shopping and she said, 'Lil girl, you only got one mama, and Nandi is not it. I am. You hear me?'" I rolled my neck in Mama Lucee fashion and mimicked her voice. "And the time when—"

"Ugh. Yes. Yes," Neveah interrupted, rising from the couch. "I remember all that. Trust me, I have many memories stored up of my mother's repugnant behaviors."

"My bad, sis." I laughed, raising my hands in surrender.

A wide smile spread across Neveah's face. "It's all good. I'm just glad to see you laughing."

She gave me a knowing look and grinned. "But I never stopped calling Nandi Momma Didi. I just didn't let my mama hear me."

"Oh, I know you didn't. And I don't blame you. Your mom is scary."

She nodded. "Very. But girl, I am going to grab my stay-ready-so-you-don't-have-to-get-ready overnight bag out of the trunk. I'm sleeping over so you don't have to be here alone tonight. TGIF."

Chapter *two*

I woke up to the unwelcoming sun spilling through my bedroom window. I threw the comforter over my face, desperately wanting to stay buried in bed, shielded away from this harsh reality.

Neveah had probably gone for an early run, knowing her. Last night, we sat up until midnight, as I drowned my sorrows quaffing wine, hoping to dull the ache in my broken heart. When I finally dragged myself to my bed, I silently cried until sleep found me.

I prayed this was just a horrible nightmare—when I awakened, I would roll out of bed and back into my normal, happy, fulfilling life with my wonderful husband. But the heaviness in my heart and deep void in the pit of my stomach was a stern reminder that I was not dreaming—I was fully awake.

Thankfully it was Saturday. I couldn't imagine making it through a workday—in the office nor at home. I wasn't scheduled for court hearings on Monday morning, so I had no last-minute case preparations to make this weekend. The mere thought of stepping inside of a courtroom or meeting with clients about family matters today—especially about divorce—turned my stomach. How was I supposed to guide anyone else with their troubles when my own had me suffocating with barely any room to breathe.

Babe, it appears that this might be a long and hectic journey for me, so as much as it pains me to say this, if you meet someone who treats you just as delicately as I have, someone who deserves you just as much, I wish you both the best whether I survive this illness or not.

I squeezed my eyes shut, shaking my head, attempting to banish the words from the letter and my husband's voice from echoing in my mind. Gable knew me. He knew how much I wanted him—how much I needed him. Why would he suggest I be with someone else? No man could fill his shoes—so big, so loving, so patient, so faithful. He had loved me all these years with unwavering devotion, selflessness—unconditionally. And now, after all this time, when life was so good, he chose to be selfish?

I screamed into my pillow, muffling my guttural cries, angry tears soaking my white satin pillowcase. I needed answers. I needed them now.

I reached for my phone, grabbing it from the nightstand. It was still on *Do Not Disturb*. After failing to reach Gable yesterday, I called his twin sister, Gabriella. No answer. I sent her a text message asking her to please call me as soon as possible, letting her know it was about Gable.

I had about a dozen new text messages waiting for me. I scrolled through them, hoping that one of them was from her. There's a message from Raymond, one of the attorneys at the firm. A few pictures from my homegirl Aurora of her extended vacation in Turks & Caicos that would soon be ending. Nothing from Gabriella.

As I continued through my text notifications, my eyes landed on a text from my little brother—my only sibling. Probably about some drama he had going on, or he needed money. I rolled my eyes and heavily sighed before reluctantly tapping it open.

Brave: *Sis, please call me when you get this, I need your help with something.*

I grimaced. "It never fails. What is it now?" I mutter to myself through clenched teeth. I shook my head. "No, I don't have time for his mess today."

This boy has been a pain in my butt and my heart since the day he was born. Frustration swelled and my chest tightened, a sharp reminder of the pain his arrival into the world caused our family—especially me and our dad. And he hadn't stopped messing up since. First, he destroyed my mother's life by taking it from her, shattering me and my dad's in the process by leaving us without her, and now he continued to mess up his own with reckless decisions.

I closed the message, turned off *Do Not Disturb,* and then scrolled through my missed calls.

My heartbeat quickened when I saw Gabriella's name in bold red letters under the missed call log. She had called me back—last night.

I hesitated before returning her call. What if she told me something I am not ready to hear? What if Gable really was sick and I was losing him forever? What if he wasn't and this was just a convenient lie to end our marriage? What if Gabriella had no idea what was going on and I invited her into our business prematurely.

Gable and I hadn't had many major problems, but we had always been mostly private and worked through our disagreements alone. Although he was close to his sister, he didn't seem to share much of our relationship challenges—if any—with her. I hadn't had any real issues with Gabriella, but we weren't close—not like sisters, not even like friends. We got along fine at family gatherings, but outside of that, we didn't talk much. She'd been a little distant ever since I'd met her. When I had asked Gable what was up with her, he assured me that it was nothing personal—that's just how she is.

As much as I wanted a closer relationship with her in the beginning of my relationship with Gable, I accepted things for what they were. I settled into the comfortable distance. The only time

Gabriella had ever truly confided in me was after their mother's funeral three years ago. That night, I'd comforted her as she vented her anger about her father. He'd jilted her mother for his mistress, building a new life once she and Gable turned eighteen years old. She'd unleashed a juxtaposition of feelings mixed with hurt and anger at his audacity to show up to their mother's funeral after not speaking to them for several years. Yet, she felt a fragile thread of relief that they might still exist in his heart, if not in his world.

Now, my mind is spun, riddled with questions about Gable's motives. Was he following in his father's footsteps? Had he abandoned me to start a family with someone else—with someone who was willing to give him something I wasn't, a child?

The ringing phone jolted me from my spiraling thoughts. I looked at the phone to see Gabriella's number flashing on the screen. She was calling me back. Before I lost the nerve, I took a deep breath in, released it, and answered the call.

"Hello," I murmured.

"Blou, hi. I got your message. Can we talk in person?"

Chapter *three*

I arrived first at the café Gabriella, and I agreed to meet at. This spot was one of my favorite places to indulge in a fancy latte. The quaint café was embellished with floral-themed decor. Soft rose petals draped the walls, accentuated by fluorescent inspiring affirmations—perfect for taking single or group photos. With cozy seating offered both inside and out, I settled on a table on the back patio. It was early spring, and the Florida weather was just right—sunny with just a light breeze passing through sporadically. The café sat along the bay side of the Gulf of Mexico. The outdoor seating offered a tranquil, serene view of the water.

Once I settled at the table, I pulled my phone out of my tote to check my emails as I waited for Gabriella to arrive. I replied to a few client emails about their upcoming custody hearings, then opened an email from Raymond. He was requesting that I take over a case previously assigned to another attorney who was suddenly placed on bedrest—two months ahead of her maternity leave. I glanced up and saw Gabriella approaching the table. The light turquoise satin matching pant set she wore complemented her flawless honey-toned skin. The wide legs of the pants flowed as she sauntered toward our table. I closed the email and slipped the cell phone back into my tote.

"Gabriella, hi." I stood to hug her. Even with the tight jawed, stern expression she wore, my sister-in-law held an undeniable beauty. Perfectly defined tight curls hung around her oval face. When our eyes met, I fought back tears as I searched the face of the woman who reminded me so much of my husband—the same almond-shaped hazel eyes, broad nose, and medium-brown complexion.

I am naturally a hugger, but I know Gabriella is not. Her body stiffened as I leaned in. I respected her space and gave her a brief, loose embrace before stepping away and settling back into my chair.

Lowering in a chair, she offered a soft smile. "I love that sundress on you, Blou," she complimented. "You look gorgeous."

I forced a smile. "Thank you. You know I love a good ol' cute and colorful Maxi dress.

She chuckled. "Yes. I love the flowers."

"You are looking quite beautiful yourself, as always," I said, offering a wink and a smile that came easier than the last.

Our eyes met for a moment as we exchanged a glance traced with sadness. A silent sorrow passed between us as we both looked away, my gaze dropping to the menu in front of me.

"Hi, ladies. What can I get for you today?"

The presence of the waitress shifted the emotional fog that had quickly hung over us, her cheerful voice cutting through the dense air.

A smile flickered across my face. "I'll have a medium hot white chocolate latte with a shot of caramel and a warm blueberry muffin, please."

"And, I will have the same drink she's having, except I'd like it iced and an avocado toast, please."

"Got it." The waitress took our menus before walking away.

My eyes settled on Gabriella.

"It's been a while. I wish we were meeting under more pleasant circumstances," I said softly.

Gabriella's face softened, her eyes sympathetic. "Yeah. So do

I." She studied my face for a few seconds before speaking again. I met her gaze, my facial expression subtle, not giving away much about how I was feeling.

"I told Gable I will meet with you, but I promised to honor his wishes. I'm sorry. I'll have to spare you the details about much of his condition, treatment, or his whereabouts."

"I sat back in my chair, folding my arms tightly across my chest.

"As his wife, you don't think I'm entitled to know every detail about what is going on with my husband?" My tone was sharp as I glared at her.

I didn't want to take my frustrations out on Gabriella, but I could feel the heat rising in me already and the conversation had just started. I expected this meeting to be a transparent heart-to-heart between us, a conversation that would lead to everything I wanted—everything I desperately needed to know—about Gable, including his whereabouts.

Gabriella cocked her head to the side. "Of course I do, Blou. I know this is hard for you. It's hard for me—hell, it's probably the hardest for Gable—but I'm only here to do what my brother asked of me."

"OK, then tell me—what is the point of meeting me if I'm going to walk away with nothing more than I came here with?"

"I can answer some of your questions, but Gable said that he will write to you weekly until he…unless he gets too weak to write. But I can fill you in on how he's doing when…if that happens."

I rolled my eyes, still sitting with my arms crossed. Struggling to keep my emotions in check, I didn't respond right away. I needed a minute to process. Fortunately, the waitress came back with our drinks and food, setting them on the table. As I stared down at my delectable-looking latte topped with whipped cream, I realized that I needed something stronger.

Gabriella waited for the waitress to walk away. Her eyes darkened with sadness. Choked with emotion, she continued, speaking slowly and calculated. "Gable has a rare illness, and the doctors don't know if he will survive it. He was chosen as a candidate for a trial study that could possibly help him beat this thing." Blinking back tears, I struggled to wrap my head around this revelation.

"Wait. How long has he known he's had this illness? He didn't seem sick to me."

"For a month. He was having mild symptoms but wasn't sure of the cause. After some bloodwork and scans, he was diagnosed. There happened to be a trial study coming up and his doctor highly recommended he participate due to how aggressive the progression could be."

"Did you know about this the entire time?" She lowered her gaze, avoiding eye contact as I glared, a single tear slipped from the corner of her eye.

"Yes. I did," She admitted. "But Blou, in his defense—"

Cutting her off, I lifted my hands, rapidly shaking my head. "No offense, Gabriella," I hissed, "but I don't think I have any tolerance for Gable's defense right now. I'm his wife, and he didn't think enough of me or have the decency to tell me about this or let me help him through it."

"I understand your frustration." She did that thing where she cocked her head to the side, again. "But that's just it, he is thinking of you. When he confided in me, I tried to convince him to tell you—that you deserved to know. He insisted that he's protecting you."

"Protecting me how?" I scoffed.

"He doesn't want you to have to watch another person you love die, nor does he want to put you in a position to have to take care of him. He knows how hard it was for you when your father—" She paused, carefully contemplating her words. Leaning in, she made steady eye contact as if to offer comfort but deliberately avoided any physical touch. "He knows how difficult it was for you helping your aunt take care of your father."

"Wow." I laughed incredulously. "All these years together, and I've never known Gable to be the controlling type—to make decisions for me."

Gabriella sighed heavily. Now it was her turn to sit back and fold her arms across her chest. Her face sank back into its former tight, stern stance. Her demeanor gave away that she was growing weary of this conversation, and my sarcasm was not making it easier.

I sighed, letting my tear-streaked face fall into my hands. I took a deep breath and exhaled before dropping my hands to the table and straightening my posture. Using a napkin from the table, I dabbed away the tears. My eyes softened as I rested them on her empty expression, wondering what she was thinking.

"Gabriella, I'm sorry. I know you're just the messenger. I'm just so angry about all of this."

To my surprise, she reached across the small table and rested her hands on mine. Empathy danced in her eyes. This gesture calmed me. It meant a lot coming from Gabriella, especially given her awkwardness to physical touch.

"Don't worry about it. I understand that this is a lot to process. Please know that Gable loves you and even if neither of us agrees with his choice, I believe he's sincerely thinking of your well-being."

"Have you been to see him at this place?" It had only been a day since he went incognito, but I ask anyway.

Pulling her hands back, she settled her elbows on the table, resting her chin on her hands. She shook her head. "No, and I won't be. No one can see him during the trial study—that's part of the contract. But I can call him. He has a landline in his room. He told me he keeps his cell phone turned off so he can focus solely on recovering with no distractions."

I didn't even ask for the number to spare the disappointment and hurt of a no.

"And..." She hesitated. "The treatment isn't in Parksdale."

Shocked, my eyes grew wide. "What? He left the city?"

"He left Florida altogether."

I opened my mouth to speak, but no words came. My heartbeat accelerated to a pounding rhythm. Panic attacks have plagued me since I was a teenager. The first one blindsided me at school right around the time we found out my dad was sick. They had become sporadic over the years, but now they'd been in a steady cycle since this dreadful situation made a grand entrance into my peaceful life.

My breathing grew labored as tears spilled from my eyes. Everything around me seemed to be spinning; my vision out of focus.

I could hear Gabriella's voice, but her words felt distant and muffled. I gasped to catch my breath, desperate for air. All the calming techniques for panic attacks that I've read on the internet now lost and foreign to me.

"Blou, breathe. Just breathe." Gabriella stood beside me, her hand resting lightly on my shoulder.

I coaxed myself to take slow, deep breaths. I closed my eyes and focused on my body—on the ground beneath my feet, the slightly cool breeze against my skin.

As my breathing slowed to a steady rhythm, I opened my eyes and quickly glanced around. The only stares were from the patrons at the table nearest us.

Still, embarrassment flushed across my hot face. I wished I could disappear into thin air and forget I'd just lost complete control of my emotions in a public setting, something that I hadn't done in years.

"Why don't we go ahead and get out of here, Blou? I know you have a lot to process. You should do something relaxing. Try to take your mind off all this for a little while." Gabriella placed her black leather handbag on her shoulder.

I nodded, knowing there would be no getting any of this off my mind any time soon. I stood and picked up my tote. Gabriella had already paid the bill and tipped the waitress.

She dug into her purse and then hands me a card. "Here is the contact number to a great therapist. It's your choice to go, of course, but I think this will be helpful for you through this process."

I scanned the card. "Thank you," finding my voice for the first time since the panic attack.

Chapter *four*

After settling in my car, once more I read the card that Gabriella had given me before placing it in the center console.

The thought of opening up with my most vulnerable feelings to a stranger was a bit unsettling. After my mom passed, I saw the school counselor a few times at my teacher's recommendation, but I never had much to say. Aunt Gina suggested I go to grief counseling after my dad passed, but she didn't force me, so I decided against it. I wasn't against therapy; I just don't know if it's right for me.

I thought back to Gabriella's words. Gable said he was doing this so I won't have to carry the burden of caring for someone else I love or watching them die.

I could admit that when my parents died, a part of me died with them. I didn't watch my mother die but losing her was no less painful than losing my father. I watched him fight cancer for two years. When the doctors told us he had six months left, that was really all he had before it took him out completely, but knowing didn't make it any easier.

My father was the strongest man I'd ever known. When my mother passed, he held our world together. He didn't hide his pain from neither me nor Brave, but he didn't allow his pain to keep him from providing a warm, secure safety net for us. He always protected us. I knew that his heart did not just break for his loss, but for me as well. He never failed to make sure I knew I mattered to him—what I felt mattered.

He understood I felt little connection to Brave. He never forced it. At times, he would delicately encourage me to take him on a walk, push him on the swings, or play with him for just a few minutes. I knew what he was doing—trying to create bonding moments between us—and I tried, mostly for him. Sometimes, I even found myself smiling at my baby brother's infectious laugh. But none of these moments were enough to erase the blame I placed on him for my mother's death.

Seeing my father sick, fragile—unlike the man I had known before the cancer, was devastating.

But still, I could not wrap my head around Gable's logic—his reason for walking away from me, his refusal to allow me the opportunity to love him through whatever this was.

We'd had endless conversations about how my parents' death scarred me—leaving me struggling with the abandonment.

Knowing all this, he still left. I don't know if I could forgive him for putting me through this.

I caught a glimpse of Neveah's name flashing on my dash screen, sweeping me from my thoughts. My phone was still in silent mode from when I met with Gabriella.

I pushed the answer button on my steering wheel.

"Hey."

"Hey, girl. Where are you?"

"In the parking lot of the café about to pull out," I said, shifting into reverse.

"I'm headed back to your place from the mall. I'm picking up Chinese from Chen's. What do you want?" Her voice blasted through the speakers.

Wincing, I turned the volume down. I forgot how loud I had been blasting my music early on the way to the café attempting to drown out the invasive thoughts about what a mess my life had become.

"Mm. I'm not really hungry."

"Well, it's not up for debate. If you can't decide, I'll just grab our usual."

"Ugh. Ok. Fine." I groaned, releasing a long sigh. "Just get me the shrimp and broccoli with shrimp fried rice and a shrimp roll."

This chick was going to be the other thorn in my side for as long as I was going through this crisis, but in a good, aggravating sister way. Neveah has always been my biggest support and she is super passionate about showing up for me when I need her. Even when I pretended I didn't.

"You already know you're stuck with me, so I don't care nothing about all that huffing and puffing," she quipped.

"Huffing and puffing?" I echoed, amused.

"Yes. Huffing and puffing," she repeated, mimicking my laugh.

"OK, mama," I joked.

"Sooo, how did the meeting with Gabriella go? I hope you got some answers."

"*Tuh*," I let out a long sigh. "Kinda. But listen, I'll talk to you when I get home—I need to call this brother of mine."

"Girl, are you sure you have the capacity to deal with whatever he has going on right now?"

"No, I'm not sure. But I also don't want him to show up on my doorstep, so I'm going to call him back."

"OK girl. See you soon."

I clicked the disconnect button on my steering wheel. I really had been trying to manage my emotions when it came to my brother.

When he was a baby, I secretly named him "the Little Thing." He was "the little thing" that took my mother away from me. I remember when I was ten years old and my father brought him home from the hospital, making a silent vow, I will never love him, never touch him, never hold him.

He cried constantly, and I hated it. His cries were a relentless reminder that he existed, and my mother didn't.

His voice was the most exasperating sound I'd ever heard. In my mind, he didn't deserve to cry. He didn't deserve to be here, so how dare he cry.

I was sure he'd always be a burden, and I wanted no parts.

As he grew older, I felt myself softening toward him, no matter how hard I tried to fight the tugs in my heart.

I couldn't help but feel something for him, but he still got under my skin.

A huge part of me still blamed him. The resentment I had towards him for having to grow up and navigate life's milestones without my mother was undeniable—my graduations, my debutante, my wedding. Each time, instead of seeing her in the audience, I saw him. Taking the spot that should have belonged to her, next to our father's sister, Aunt Georgina, or as we call her, Aunt Gina. She helped my father take care of us after my mother's death. After we lost our father, she didn't hesitate to embrace the full tutelary responsibilities of caring for us. She and Uncle Lance both loved us unconditionally and are still our strongest supporters.

I could hear Aunt Gina's voice in my head:

"Blou, your mother's death was very unfortunate and tragic—It rocked every one of our worlds. You are entitled to your feelings, but her death is not your brother's fault. Remember, that he did not ask to be born, and he certainly didn't ask to be born into a big world without a mother to care for him."

I heard this spiel from her a million times. Logically speaking, I knew Aunt Gina was right, and I was trying, but it was easier said than done.

I took a long deep breath and slowly exhaled before I voice commanded my phone to call Brave.

"Hey, big sis," Brave answered on the first ring, his tone lit up with enthusiasm.

I braced myself, willing away the irritation I always felt anytime he called me or showed up unannounced on my doorstep—

anytime I saw him, period. Keeping my voice steady, I said, "hey, what's up?"

"I was wondering if I can come over so we can talk face-to-face. I have an idea I think you might like."

I rolled my eyes. I almost never liked any of Brave's "ideas," so I doubted I would like this one—he never even followed through. I'd grown tired of his random, off-the-wall pipe dreams.

"I know what you're going to say." Sensing my hesitation, he jumped in, hurriedly before I could respond. "Just…hear me out before you say anything."

I sat in silence, contemplating whether to shut him down from the jump or accede to his request to hear him out.

"Pleassse," he pleaded.

Against my better judgment, I acquiesced. "OK. You can come by tomorrow afternoon."

"Great. Thank you." His excitement was palpable.

I paused for a bit before reminding him of my boundaries. "And Brave—"

"Huh?"

"Afternoon. Not evening. Understood?"

"Yeah, yeah, sis. I got it. I love you. Thank you."

"Mm-hmm. Bye," I mumbled disconnecting the call before he could say anything else.

Chapter *five*

"Girl, this is some heavy stuff," Neveah said after I filled her in on my conversation with Gabriella.

"Tell me about it," I agreed, letting out a sigh. It was just early evening, and I was already feeling the exhaustion of the day.

We sat in the gathering room, the remnants of our early dinner scattered across the coffee table—Neveah's empty Chinese take-out box, and mine, half-full. She had baked chocolate chip cookies, plated them on a serving tray and placed them close by on the end table.

We opted for water and tea today since last night I'd desperately guzzled wine like I was going to find some sanity at the bottom of the bottle. I am not a regular drinker, but somehow, I managed to wrap up my entire weekend alcohol limit within a couple of hours.

We sat comfortably on the couch. Neveah was cocooned in my favorite off-white plush faux fur blanket, while half my body was covered to my waist with Gable's black and dark gray mink blanket, my legs stretched out parallel to hers.

"You know what you need?" Neveah asked, a sly grin playing

on her face.

I shook my head. "Neveah, I don't want any parts of whatever shenanigans you have up your devious sleeves."

"Who said my shenanigans are devious? Girl, I'm an angel who's going to make sure you have some fun for a change. You are always either working, up under Gable—no shade—holed up at home with a book to your face or crocheting—again, no shade."

"OK, and? Those are the things that make me happy."

"And I'm not saying they don't, but you need to have some good unwholesome fun sometimes."

"Girl, you know I'm not going to a club."

"Now, Blou, you know I don't just go to any ol' club. I only do grown and sexy jazz lounges like the one downtown on Wellington Ave. But I'm not talking about clubbing. Let's go away—a little girls trip. Just me, you, and Ro."

"Mm. I have work, and Aurora is still on her trip. She sent me pictures last night."

"Girl, please. Just check your calendar for next weekend. Aurora will be back tomorrow. I spoke to her last night, and she's down."

"Did you tell her…about Gable?"

"I didn't go into any details. This is your story to tell, my friend, but I told her we have a Code 14 in progress, then I pitched the trip."

I really didn't mind if Neveah had told Ro. It saved me from the emotional toll of retelling everything myself. Besides, they had both been sisters I'd never had since eighth grade.

By the time we went off to Howard University for college, our bonds had only grown tighter. The cozy and safe feelings of camaraderie surrounding our friendship made it so much easier as I navigated the loss of my father, and even as I still grieved my mother and wrestled with feelings of animosity toward my brother.

In middle school, Neveah put Code 14 in place as a distress alert when it seemed like one of us was slipping into a self-pity party or had been in a bout of self-pity too long. She had always been anti-pity party, and that hadn't changed.

A trip wasn't really a bad idea. I hadn't been on one with my girls in three years. Not because I did not want to, but I had gotten into the groove of my day-to-day life, and honestly, I'd grown content there.

"Let me check my calendar, and I'll get back to you," I said.

"Um, ma'am. I'm pretty sure you can check your calendar right now and go ahead and block off that time if it's available. You aren't fooling me."

I rolled my eyes. "*Tuh*. You know what? Fine. It probably is a good idea if I check now because I don't need you hounding me every hour," I said, grabbing my phone.

The second I unlocked it, I saw a text message notification from Brave.

*Looking forward to our talk tomorrow. *Beaming face with smiling eyes emoji.**

I frowned and backed out of the message without responding.

"Ugh. Why are you looking like someone just pissed on your brand-new Louboutin heels?" Neveah quipped.

"Chile, it's nothing. Just Brave messaging me," I muttered, eyes scanning my calendar.

"Ah, Ok." She laughed.

"Actually, my calendar is clear for next Thursday and Friday."

"Perfect! I'll book the flights," she said, with a toothy smile, excitement glowing on her face.

"Wait, just wait one minute. Where are we going?" I raised a brow, tilting my head.

"Well…um…"

"Neveahhh. Where?"

"I know you said you didn't do reunions, but—"

"Ooh, no. You're talking about going to that Howard mixer for the classes of 2016 and 2017? Nope. I'm not going to that," I protest, raising my hands and rapidly shaking my head."

"Please, Blou. It'll be fun and why not go to this one since you've already decided against the ten-year reunion."

"Girl, have you forgotten what I'm dealing with right now? Do you think I want to go to a college mixer and face all those nosey, fake people asking personal questions about my life?"

"Since when do you care about what people think?" she shot back. "And who says you need to answer to anyone? We're just going to enjoy ourselves. It will be cool to visit the old stomping grounds too. Neither of us has been back since graduation."

"Yeah, eight years is a long time. I haven't been back to DC at all since moving back home to Parksdale," I added quietly.

"Ahhh. I see what's going on here. You are afraid of running into—"

"Don't." My voice was sharp, cutting her off before she said his name.

"Zamir," she blurted anyway, smirking.
I shot a fierce glare her way. If my eyes could burn, she would be blazing.

She burst into laughter. "The look on your face is a dead give-away that you are still not over that man."

"The look on my face tells you no such a thing." I felt a tinge of sadness at the thought of him. So many good memories that outweighed the bad, but a trace of pain still touched the surface.

"Girl, it's ok. Most people will always feel something for their first love. He was your college sweetheart. Y'all would probably still be together now if he hadn't stayed up North after college."

My glare intensified with every word she spoke. I was not going to discuss Zamir. I had always felt that we were each other's lost love, but we were young. I moved on, got married, and the last I heard, so had he. Well, the last Aurora told me she saw on his social media since I'd blocked him. He didn't post much but she saw that he had changed his status from single to married. After that, I told her not to tell me anything else. I had him blocked for a reason.

But none of that mattered. I was happy—or at least I had been. I met Gable right after I moved back home. We dated for a little over two months before we were exclusive. Eight months after

Zamir and I broke up, I was married. Neveah thought I was moving on too fast. Ro gave me a spiel about life being too short, so go for it. And I did.

"Next subject." I scowled. My husband could possibly die. I was not about to sit here and unpack my past relationship with an old lover.

Neveah hesitated, her eyes searching my face, likely, trying to decide whether to push the conversation about Zamir forward or leave it where it was.

Not giving her a chance to decide, I pivoted to another topic—this time, about her.

"So…are you going to marry Lukas?" I asked, eyebrows arched as I waited for her answer.

Now it was her turn to burn a hole in my face with the fire in her eyes. Her eyes locked with mine. I held her gaze, staring back at her.

She sighed dramatically, falling back onto the couch, burying her face in her hands. "Girl, I don't know," She groaned. "I love him so much, but I really have to think this thing through. Marriage is forever."

"Mmm. Yeah, that's what I thought too," I murmured and lowered my gaze.

Neveah sat up straight. She reached over and placed a comforting hand on mine. "Honey, your situation is very unique. Things like this don't happen every day. One thing I know—regardless of what happens with Gable—you are going to be fine."

Tears welled in my eyes. I slowly shook my head as if to shake away any thoughts about Gable.

I looked up at my best friend and forced a smile that didn't quite reach my eyes. "Let's talk about this trip."

Chapter Six

This morning was tough. I woke up feeling like darkness surrounded my empty heart. Getting out of bed meant facing another round of hard truths and inescapable facts I wasn't ready to face.

Ms. Anti-Pity Party was not having it. Neveah all but dragged me out of bed and into the shower. Coffee and a light breakfast of avocado toast, scrambled eggs and a medley of berries was waiting for me on the breakfast nook when I got to the kitchen.

"Have you thought about seeing a therapist?" she asked casually as we sat at the breakfast nook, her eyes fixed on her phone.

I gave a quick shake of my head. "No. Ironically, Gabriella gave me a card to a therapist she recommends. I just don't think therapy is for me."

"It helped me after my breakup with Derrick. I think you should consider it." She glanced over at me. "I still have my therapist on speed dial just in case I need her."

I took a bite of avocado toast as I mulled over what Neveah said. I knew how much therapy helped her, but everyone's different.

She was about to say something else when the doorbell rang.

She paused. "Are you expecting someone?"

I frowned. "Mm. No."

I grabbed my phone to check the camera app. Letting out a long frustrated sigh, I scowled. "It's Brave."

"Oh, but you told him to come by today, right?"

"This afternoon. Not this morning. Not this evening. This afternoon. The boy has zero respect for boundaries."

I lifted myself from the stool to go open the door.

"Well, I'm going to leave you two to whatever business you have. I have to meet up with Lukas." She followed me to the door, grabbing her crossbody from the couch.

"You mean whatever tomfoolery this boy has going on," I muttered.

"Girl, relax and give him a chance. This might be something good this time. Give him grace. I love you." She wrapped me in a hug and stepped past me, unlocking and pulling open the door.

Brave stood tall, a wide grin stretched across his face. I scanned his attire. He wore a pair of dark slacks, a light-colored t-shirt, a dark blazer matching his pants, and black casual sneakers.

I quietly giggled to myself when I noticed he held a black portfolio. *This kid really is extra*, I thought.

"Heyyyy, little brother!" Neveah said, grinning. "Looking good." She pulled him into a tight hug. "Good to see you."

"Heeeyyy Sis." He grinned back, returning her embrace. "Good seeing you too."

Neveah turned to me, gave me a wink, and called over her shoulder, "I'll catch you later." Brave watched in amusement as she strolled down the walkway to her dark red Benz.

I waved as she pulled out of the driveway.

"I can't wait until I am driving a fancy whip like that." His eyes lit up.

"Mm. You did once, but you wrecked it, remember?" I muttered through clenched teeth, more critical than I intended.

He seemed to be ignoring my tone. "Yeah, that is when I was eighteen—young, reckless, and immature. I'm a twenty-two-year-old grown man now." He flashed a wide, goofy grin.

I rolled my eyes. "Boy, please. Get on in here." I turned away and headed toward the kitchen.

Following closely, he started rapping some song I'm sure he made up because I'd never heard it before.

I spun to face him. "This better not be another ploy to get me to invest into some so called 'rap career' again," I said, complete with air quotations.

He chuckled. "I wouldn't even waste your time. That ship has sailed."

"Good. Then let's get this over with. What is it?" I stood with a hand resting on each hip.

"Dang. Can I at least get something to drink first and some of this fancy avocado toast?"

"Boy, this is barely fancy, but help yourself," I said, fighting a giggle, and smiling just a little.

I stood by the island as he spread avocado onto a slice of toast and took a seat on a stool, his eyes wandering. "Where's Gable? Is the data scientist in his office immersed in some nerdy computer programing stuff?" he asked with a smirk.

My smile faded. "Mm. No. He's not here. Let's focus on why you're here," I snapped.

He raised his hands. "Ookay. I'm sorry I asked. Trouble in paradise?"

I hesitated.

I had been so caught up in my own down spiraling and heartbreak that I didn't even think about Gable's work. When we met, I should have asked Gabriella about their plans. She and Gable ran their late mother's tech company. Would she be able to run it without him? I made a mental note to call her after Brave left.

My gaze narrowed. "Why are you here?"
A grimace of pain crossed his face; he lowered his eyes and cleared his throat but said nothing.

Noticing his expression, I immediately regretted how harsh my tone had been.

"I'm sorry," I softened. "I didn't mean to come across—"

"Mean," he said quietly, lifting his eyes to meet mine. "It's no big deal. I'm used to it."

My eyes dropped, and guilt settled in my chest.

"But, I'll get right to it, so you can get back to your life," he said, sarcasm dripping from his words.

I couldn't even be offended. I had been nothing but cold to him since he'd walked through the door. Something about him did that to me.

Truth is, I knew why. I couldn't ignore how much I wished my mom was here instead of him.

Or maybe… I wanted them both to be here. I just couldn't shake this disdain I had toward him.

I felt a heaviness creeping up in my chest. *Oh no.* I thought. My heart quickened. *I cannot have a panic attack. Not in front of Brave.*

I tried my hardest to shove the emotions down, but the harder I tried, the harder it was to breathe. My fingers gripped the edge of the counter, as I struggled to slow my breathing.

"Are you OK?" I could feel Brave suddenly beside me, I hadn't even noticed he moved. I could feel my body trembling, slightly, barely noticeable. "Yeah…Yeah...Yeah…I…I."

Brave placed a firm but gentle hand on my back. "Sis, just breathe. I got you."

Tears spilled hot down my cheeks as my breathing slowed.

As my heart rate steadied, I realized my brother was standing over me—witnessing me in a full-blown panic attack. I felt my face flush with embarrassment.

My eyes darted, avoiding eye contact. "I'm sorry, I—"

"You don't need to apologize. I know what panic attacks are like."

My eyes met his gaze. "You have panic attacks?" My brows furrowed.

"Yes. Well, I used to. I haven't had one in almost a year. My therapist helped me to manage them, and honestly, the more we talked the less they happened."

I blinked. "Your therapist? You go to therapy?" This conversation was becoming more interesting by the second.

He chuckled. "Been going for about a year and a half now."
"Oh."
"You sure you're OK, sis?" he asked.
His five-foot-ten frame shadowed my five-foot six-inch stance. I glanced up and for a second, I was caught off guard by his resemblance to mom. His warm caramel complexion, those big, brown eyes we both inherited stared back at me laced with empathy. The concern etching his face mirrored hers when I would get sick, or sad about anything.

We had never exchanged this kind of vulnerability before. I had never allowed space for it. It was unfamiliar. Awkward. Yet, surprisingly, a flicker of warmth settled in my chest. Discovering an unexpected commonality between us wove a quiet thread of connection—very fragile, but real, nonetheless.

Straightening, I cleared my throat, steadying my voice. "Um. Yes. I'm fine."

I grabbed two bottles of water from the island, motioning toward the gathering room. "Come. Let's go sit."

I settled onto the couch; Brave chose the recliner. I twisted the cap off my water bottle, took a sip, and waited patiently for him to pitch the idea that he was so adamant about. I was pretty sure whatever he needed from me would be a hard no.

"So…" he started then hesitated, fidgeting absentmindedly with a rubber band he wore around his wrist.

I frowned, confused about why he was wearing a rubber band but quickly refocused my attention—after all it was Brave. Nothing had to make sense when it came to him.

I swore I could see a flicker of nervousness in his demeanor. That would be a first. Brave was never nervous about anything.

"Well," he spoke again, "I have an idea for an app."

"OK. What does that have to do with me exactly?" I narrowed my eyes, suspicious about where this was going. This already seemed like it was going to be a joke.

"I want to create a social media app focusing on cryptocurrency." He pushed the words out quickly before losing courage.

I simply stared at him. Another "bright idea" that would be

added to his growing list of failures. But after the fiasco in the kitchen—his non-judgmental support—I decided to choose my words carefully. I really didn't want to hurt his feelings, but I needed clarity.

"Again, what does that have to do with me?" I raised an eyebrow.

"I would like for you to invest in it," he said, this time with a little more confidence.

Without thinking, I let out a giggle. "What? You must be sick." I got up, walked over and pressed the back of my hand to his forehand like I was checking for a fever.

He swatted my hand away. "Blou, come on. I'm serious." His expression hardened.

"Oh, you're for real." I laughed again, sinking back on the couch.

"Why are you laughing?" he pushed, his tone pleading. "I think it's a great business idea. It can make big money. I will pay you back when it does. I promise."

"Brave, have you forgotten the amount of money I've already loaned you? Money, I haven't gotten back?"

"I know. I don't deny that. I know you've poured a significant amount of money into my dreams. I can admit that my dreams have changed a thousand times, but this is the one, sis. I can feel it. The game changer."

I was not convinced. He'd said that about every so-called game changer that flamed out before it got off the ground.

"I'm pretty sure you've burned through most, if not all, of your inheritance and some of mine with your so-called game changers, Brave. I don't know. I just—"

"Listen," he said, leaning in, locking his eyes with mine, "this is different. I've done the research. I've written out a plan. I'm ready for this. I'm committed. I even had Tyrek to help me."

"Tyrek?" I asked, disgust thick in my tone.

"Yes. He's been helping me."

I blinked. "You mean the same Tyrek who helped you into debt the last time? Yeah, no. I am not investing into anything that man has his scandalous hands in."

He chuckled. "Tyrek is not scandalous. He's made some mistakes, but he's not some criminal mastermind." He shook his head.

"Um, if you say so, but I'm not convinced that guy is legit with anything he does. He even looks shady." I cringed at the image of him in my head. "He always has this…sideways grin. And nothing is worse than those firm sweaty handshakes."

Brave smacked his forehead and groaned—an amused smile playing on his lips. "You are a trip. Look, if it helps, I assure you, Tyrek is not a partner or anything close. Not this time. He knows a lot about this kind of business. He answered some questions I had and just helped me get the paperwork and contract together and introduced me to some vendors, because he knows some people. Nothing more."

I sat quietly, letting the silence fill the room again. Maybe I was a fool to even be considering this. Curiosity tugged at me. "And just how much do you need from me for this bright idea?"

"Twenty-five thousand," he said without blinking.

My eyes widened.

"But," he rushed, "once the money starts coming in—and I know it will—I can also pay you back all the other money you've loaned me."

He reached over taking my hands in his. "Please."

I looked at his hands covering mine. We had never been the hand-holding type of siblings. Awkwardness made its way to the pit of my stomach triggering those annoying somersaults that had become common lately. I slowly pulled away. Too much.

I exhaled sharply, forcing my eyes toward him.

"I promise I have it all figured out, Blou. Just give me this one last chance to prove it to you."

I pulled my bottom lip into my mouth and lightly nibbled on it. "I need more time to think about this."

"Understandable." He stretched the leather portfolio out in front of me. "Here. Take a look."

"Mm. Ok. Fancy," I teased, taking the folder from his hand. I flipped it open half-way expecting to see nothing but handwritten, unorganized chaos. As I skimmed over the documents inside, I was impressed. They were professional and well written—polished. Brave was intelligent, no doubt. That had never been the issue. The issue was he never follows through with anything he started. He swiftly jumped from one "great idea" to the next, recklessly burning through money. The only reason he probably had any money left at all was because Aunt Gina promised my father to hold on to most of it until he turned twenty-five. The same she'd done for me, except I had access to more since I was in college. Brave had a car and condo that was paid for. His entry-level job in IT kept money in his pocket for necessities and to play around with.

Yet the more I read, the more my doubt and skepticism wavered. His business plan had structure. It seemed like this time, he had actually thought this plan through.

Despite the utter frustration—and the quiet resentment—I couldn't seem to shake, his attempt to cajole me was working. I truly did want him to succeed. Whatever my personal feelings toward him, I knew my parents well. If nothing else, they would have wanted us both to thrive and successfully stand on our own.

But if I decided to help him this would without a doubt be the last time. If he messed this up, he was on his own. No more bailouts.

Locking eyes with my brother, I said, "Tell me more."

Chapter *Seven*

I sat curled up in the oversized chaise in my bedroom, wrapped in a blanket, savoring a warm cup of Chamomile tea, staring out of the large bay window. Orange and gold hues spread across the skyline—the setting sun emulated a soft glow over the horizon.

My mind wandered to Gable. After we purchased this house, this had become our favorite spot in the evening. We spent countless nights lying here tangled together, watching the sunset, sharing stories about our day, laughing at each other's corny jokes, and planning out a future I thought was certain.

After Brave left, I called Gabriella and asked her if she would be running the business alone while Gable was out…healing, I suppose. She assured me they had worked everything out and she had it all under control. I pushed for more answers, to no avail.

I swelled with frustration after hanging up with her. She was noticeably short with me during the call. I understood her loyalty was to her brother, but I needed more answers. I feel powerless, Gable made decisions about both our lives—present and future—leaving me with no voice in the matter. I felt stuck in uncertainty, a heavy weight pressing on me. Something had to give—and fast—before I lost my mind.

I released a long, breathy sigh as I pushed myself from the chaise. As much as I didn't have an appetite, I needed to eat something. I remembered the leftover Chinese food from yesterday.

I made my way down the hall toward the kitchen. As I passed Gable's office door, I stopped and turned toward it. His office was one room in the house I rarely went into.

I rested my fingers on the knob and hesitated before turning it, halfway expecting the door to be locked. I don't know why because he never locked it, but with so many secrets and unexpected surprises, I wasn't sure what to expect anymore.

I stepped into the office, my gaze taking in how spotless and well-organized Gable kept it. Every item was meticulously placed. His bookshelves, desk, every small detail were well thought out.

As I stood there, flashbacks of the day we moved in surfaced. The movers had come and gone, leaving everything in place—except this room, still waiting to be furnished.

Vivid memories stirred of us romantically consummating the empty space. Our bodies pressed against the wall, and then on the floor tangled in a passionate knot, lost in the heat of each other's embrace—in our own world where only we existed.

I shivered, shaking off the invasive thoughts. I sauntered over to the mahogany L-shaped desk and eased in the brown leather ergonomical chair.

Scanning the items on the desk, I realized that I had no idea what I was looking for. But I needed to look. Something—anything—with some hint of where Gable really was. I still didn't fully buy the story about him just running off to a trial study out of state. Sure, Gabriella backed his story. I'd never known her to lie—but like she said, her loyalty was to her brother.

I tugged one of the drawers on the desk. Locked. I tried the rest. The last drawer slid open. Empty. There was an oversized desk calendar laying on the top of the desk. Lifting it, I checked beneath for a key. Nothing. *Weird*, I thought. Why would he have locked the other drawers?

I pressed the power button on the computer and watched as the screen lit up. At the password prompt, I entered the standard password—the one we both used across our devices and accounts. Password failed.

I frowned.

I could feel frustration prickle under my skin, my cheeks warming.

I tried another password. Failed again.

Deciding not to try a third time and risk getting locked out altogether, I rested my elbows on the desk, chin in my hands. My fingers tapped against the side of my face, partly to soothe myself, partly thinking. Something wasn't right.

I turned to face the massive mahogany bookshelf that lined the entire wall behind the desk filled with books, trinkets, and whatnots. I opened one of the lower cabinet doors. A safe. Matte black. Keypad entry. Interesting.

I had no idea Gable had a safe other than the one we shared in one of our bedroom closets.

I was in deep thought when a light knock on the door pulled me out of it. Startled, I swiveled around in the chair to see Neveah's head poking through the cracked door.

"Hey," she said, scanning the room. "What you got going on in here?"

I let out a long sigh and sank back into the chair. "Girl, you scared the crap out of me. I didn't hear you come in."

"Hmm. Maybe because you are snooping. I've been back for about thirty minutes. You were in your room, so I didn't want to disturb you."

I shot her a side eye. "Snooping? In my own house? *Tuh*. Please."

She chuckled, walking deeper into the office. "OK, then. What did you find?"

"Mmph. I found a whole safe that I didn't even know was here. Girl, how can I not know what's in my own house?"

Neveah frowned. "Maybe because this is your husband's office that you barely step foot in because you never have a reason too." There's probably plenty in here you don't know about.

"Well, thank you, Neveah. That's super helpful," I said with thick sarcasm in my voice.

"Blou, I didn't mean that in a bad way. There just might be a lot of things in here you've never seen."

"Yeah, but a safe is something I should have known about—something Gable should have told me about."

She nodded in agreement.

"And that's not all."

She raised an eyebrow and leaned in the way she always did when she is anticipating gossip. "What else?"

"You know we use the same passwords across all of our devices, right?" I asked rhetorically.

"Yeah, in case something happens to one of you and you need to get into the accounts. You always said that was important to the two of you."

"Correct."

"OK?"

"I tried to log in to his computer and the password failed."

"Whaat? That's wild, sis."

"Tell me about it. Not only did I find a safe and I'm locked out of his computer, but the desk drawers are also all locked."

Neveah stood quietly, glancing around the room.

"I wonder what he's hiding," I mumbled, partially to myself.

"I don't know. You know I'm not going to sugarcoat. Something does seem off."

I couldn't find any more words. I was dumbfounded that Gable was hiding things from me. We never hid things from each other. I don't know why anything was shocking to me anymore after he hid a freaking rare illness and disappeared, leaving me only an empty letter promising to write again.

The more I thought about Gable keeping secrets from me after he'd promised me commitment, honesty and loyalty, the more anger metastasized through my body, pushing tension into my neck and shoulders, threatening a headache. I could feel a dull ache beginning to intensify across my entire head.

"*Arrggh*! I am so angry! I yelled, slamming my fists against the surface of the desk.

With celerity, I swiped my arms across the desk, sending pens, papers, the calendar—everything—crashing to the floor.

I reached for the computer, ready to thrust it to the carpet along with everything else when Neveah yelled my name.

"Blou! Stop it." Her sharp command snapped me out of my fury.

I snatched my hands back from the computer. Not knowing what to do with them, I wrapped them around myself. A river of tears flooded my face.

She walked over to me and wrapped her arms around me, holding me tightly. My body went limp in her embrace. Sobbing uncontrollably, I released a fierce wail. The intense flow of emotions quickly drained what little energy I had left. My legs buckled. I slid to the floor, bringing Neveah with me.

Leaning against the desk, now sobbing softly, I rested my head on her shoulder. It felt like something inside of me was breaking, a reminder of what the chokehold of loss once did to my spirit— my heart.

Neveah sat in silence, rubbing my shoulder and rocking us both at a slow, steady pace, welcoming a serene quietude as the dark cloud of indignation gradually lost its grip.

Sitting up straight, I reached over and grabbed the box of Kleenex that I had knocked to the floor during my rage. I pulled two pieces of tissue from the box and handed them to Neveah. I didn't need to look at her to know she was crying while holding me together. I had heard her sniffles.

I took two more tissues for myself, wiped my face and blew my nose, then I looked over at my friend.

"Thank you for being here."

"Of course," she said, wiping tears from her cheeks. "I know it's hard right now, but you're going to get through this, and I'll be here every step of the way. I promise."

"Yeah," I said, quietly. I know."

"Listen. Since you're already taking Thursday and Friday off for our trip, are you able to push all this week's stuff to next week—

take the week to clear your head? Unless you have court?"

"I don't have any hearings this week, but I do have depositions to prepare for."

"You can do that from home, right?"

I nodded slowly. "Yeah. That's actually not a bad idea."

"Good." She smiles.

She was right about taking time off. I really wasn't in the mental head space to meet with colleagues or clients. I needed time to sort out some of this chaos—get my thoughts together.

I rose from the floor and held out a grateful hand to help Neveah up. Not needing the help, she took it anyway. As I pulled her on her feet, we both laughed, despite the tears that still streaked down both our faces.

"I need to check in with Fallon—have her bring some files over and push back the few meetings I have to next week," I said, settling into the chair.

I picked up my phone and opened the work calendar. Luckily, I didn't have many meetings with clients scheduled, only colleagues. I marked the days as *Out of Office* so nothing else is added, then I called my assistant.

"Hey, Mrs. Rivers-Whitmore," she answered, chipper as usual.

I sighed, rolling my eyes. "Fallon, how many times have I told you to call me by my first name when we aren't in meetings?"

She giggled. "Oops. Right. What can I do for you, Blou?"

Fallon reminded me of myself ten years ago—ambitious, sharp and eager to learn. She was fresh out of college when I hired her. She had been my assistant for a year and a half and still hadn't broken the habit of calling me by my last name unnecessarily. She was an exceptional assistant though. Punctual, confident, and always a step ahead.

"First of all, I hope you are having a wonderful weekend," I said.

"I most certainly am. To what do I owe the pleasure of a weekend call?"

I normally didn't bother Fallon on the weekends unless we had some kind of prep work we needed to get done by Monday.

"I'm glad your weekend is good. Listen, I've decided to work from home this week. Tomorrow, I need you to bring me the Johnson, Washington, and Hunter files. Also, please push my meetings with Raymond and Jared to next week."

"Will do, boss. Raymond did mention he has a new case he needs to transfer to you from Kerry since she's out on maternity leave."

"Yes, I read the email. It'll have to wait until I return to the office, or he can assign it to someone else if it's urgent."

The line was silent for a few seconds.

"Um. Is everything OK? You never take a week off abruptly like this," she said, concern in her voice.

Fallon might be my assistant, but I've grown to love her like family, and I knew she felt the same. I was grateful for her concern, but I would rather keep the details about what was going on with Gable between close friends—at least for now.

"Yes. I just have some personal things going on. Can you come by before noon—around ten-thirty?"

"Got it. Is there anything else I can do to help?"

"No. I'm fine. Thank you. I will let you know if anything else comes up. See you in the morning."

"Wait, Blou."

"Yes?"

"Tell Brave I said heyyyy?"

I frowned. "Mm. Girl, no."

She laughed. "He's so fine, though."

"OK, now. I've told you he is not the one for you. Trust me on this. Warning comes before destruction. I'll see you tomorrow. Goodbye."

"Alright, alright. Focus on myself. Got it." She giggled. "Goodbye, boss. See ya."

I disconnected the call, shaking my head, smiling to myself. Fallon had met Brave at an office party he begged me to let him attend last year. Since then, she had been asking about him constantly and he'd asked about her a few times. They would probably be a great match for each other if he had his act together, but he didn't, so that is out of the question.

Neveah was browsing around on Gable's bookshelf. She pulled a book out and read the title. *"Parenthood: Deciding to Have a Baby: You're Ready, She's Not.* "Hmmm. Interesting," She glanced at me, then back at the book.

"What? Let me see that." I stood and took the book from her, eyeing the cover. Reality hit me like a ton of bricks.

Neveah spoke aloud what I was thinking. "That man really wanted a baby, girl—like really bad."

"I know," I said, barely above a whisper. "I just can't. I couldn't." I shook my head.

Gable and I had many discussions about having a child before we got married. Prior to marrying me, he knew about my fears of becoming pregnant. He knew that was not an option for me. Ever. I never led him to believe there was ever a possibility. Throughout our marriage, he would bring it up—check in to see if anything changed but he never pushed.

Still, a part of me knew he desperately wanted a baby, but I never knew he was reading books about it. He must have thought about it a lot.

I always knew he would be a wonderful father. I just couldn't fulfill that part of his life. Maybe I was selfish to marry him knowing this. He said he wanted *me* more, but this made me wonder if he was as happy as he claimed to be.

Maybe, even if he survived this illness, I didn't deserve for him to come back. Maybe I never deserved to have him.

Guilt filled my chest, and a sudden pang of nausea riddled my stomach. I could feel those darn somersaults rising deep in my gut again. My heart raced. I blinked rapidly as tears filled my eyes, but I refused to let them fall.

Neveah must have sensed the panic.

"Hey." Her voice was soft, eyes empathetic as she gently took the book from my hands and placed it back in its cozy home on the shelf. "How about we go watch a movie or something?

She nudged me, shoulder to shoulder. Then, she linked her arm through mine like she always did when words weren't enough.

"As long as it's a comedy. I need a good laugh."

She smiled. "I'll pop the popcorn. You grab the cheese and crackers."

Chapter *eight*

Since I'd begrudgingly rolled out of bed, made a cup of coffee as a quick breakfast substitute, and sat down at my desk, I've not been able to get that safe off my mind.

After Fallon dropped the files off, I tried to focus. I hadn't gotten much done in the three hours that I'd been working but still, I decided I needed a break.

I picked up my phone and strolled through my notifications. I had a missed call from Aunt Gina. Judging by the time stamp, she had called yesterday, right around the time of my meltdown. Since I'd missed our weekly Sunday call, I hope she wasn't thinking something is off with me. Even though things were very off. And I have been kind of avoiding her. Aunt Gina seems to have a sixth sense of some sorts. It's like she knew when something was not right with me or Brave.

As I continued scrolling my notifications, I saw that I had a text from Brave. I opened it.

Brave: *Good morning, sis. I wanted to thank you again for helping me out. I promise I will not let you down.*

Me: *I'm not going
to say you're welcome until I see it with my own eyes. Remember,
do not sign anything at all until I say so. I'm going to have an
attorney at my office look everything over first. Understood?*

Brave: *No problem. Understood.*

Me: *I'm out of the office for the week, but I'll talk to him as soon
as I get back next Monday.*

Brave: *Aw. A whole week?*

Me: *Yes. Just be patient.*

Brave: *Alrighty. But why are you off this week? Are you going on
vacation? Where are you going?*

Me: *Something like that. And touch your nose. I will call you next
week.*

Brave: *You never take a vacation with me.*

Me: *Bye, Brave.*

I watched the typing dots pulse on the screen, waiting for his
next reply.
The dots disappeared.
The reply never came.
I didn't want to hurt his feelings, but I could barely take being
around him in small doses, let alone a whole vacation. Vacations
were for relaxing. For the little time were in the room together on
sporadic occasions his presence kept me emotionally charged, on
edge, and overwhelmed—nowhere near relaxed.
It was anxiety-inducing enough to have invested such a large
sum of money into that cryptocurrency app, especially not knowing if it would succeed. One thing that did give me confidence in

my decision was having a trusted colleague look over everything. I would know if it was legit before any contracts were signed.

I exited the message thread, then dialed Aunt Gina's number.

"Hey there, Blou Bear," she chirped.

A half smile gave in to her warm, inviting voice. My eyes watered as I longed for her loving embrace right now.

"Hey Auntie. How are you?" I pushed the words out, aiming for a cheerful tone but falling short as my voice cracked.

"I'm doing fine. Are you OK, baby? You sound a little down."

"I'm fine—just a little tired. How's Uncle Lance?" I rushed to change the subject before she could pry.

I was never good at lying to anyone, especially to her. There was no need to burden her with my problems when I didn't know much myself. I wouldn't be the only reason she would worry. She and Gable had a close-knit relationship. He was like a son to her.

She hesitated before answering as if she wanted to push more but decided to let it go. "He's doing good. A little under the weather with a cold but nothing too bad."

"Aw. I hope he feels better soon. I know you're taking good care of him."

"Yes. It's like taking care of an ailing baby, but I'm managing." She chuckled.

Releasing a short giggle, I pictured my uncle in bed dramatically groaning while Aunt Gina rolled her eyes as she fluffed his pillows and spoon fed him homemade chicken noodle soup.

I loved how my aunt and uncle loved on each other. They had been me and Brave's blueprint for a healthy example of love. I do not know where Brave got his toxic tendencies. We both had the same examples of a loving marriage. He was young and reckless, which was why I could never let him drag Fallon and her fragile heart into his chaos. She was too good of an assistant, and most importantly, too good of a person. I would hate for her to be collateral damage.

"How's Gable?" Aunt Gina's soft voice nudged me back into the conversation. Her question plunged deep to my core, twisting my stomach into knots.

"*Um*. He's fine." Grasping for redirection, I blurted, "Are you sure Unc will be well enough to grill for the annual family cook out?

I am looking forward to his famous fall-off-the-bone ribs."

She laughed heartily. "Of course. You know he's already been talking about it every chance he gets to anyone who listens. I'm really looking forward to spending time with you, your brother, and Gable. He's going to love this new pie recipe I've been perfecting. I know you all are busy, but I wish all of you would visit more."

"I know, Auntie. I'll try to get over there more often."

"Brave did come by here this past weekend. He was excited about some crypto…something. Said you were helping him with it."

I laughed. "Cryptocurrency, Auntie. I did agree to help him, but honestly, I'm not sure I'm making the right decision. Brave has a habit of screwing up everything he gets his hands on."

"Aw. Now I think it's a great idea. That boy went on and on about his plans and ideas for this thingamajig. You know you just have to be patient with him, Blou. He really does try so hard to make you proud. Always did seek your approval."

I snorted. "Well, he better not mess up this time, or I'm done with him for good." I ignored her comment about him seeking my approval. I never really thought about that, and I certainly didn't want to get into that conversation right now—or ever, if I was being honest.

"Oh, you don't mean that, baby. I know you've struggled for years with your relationship with your brother, but he really means well. He has a kind heart, just like you—just like both your mother and father did."

"Mm-hm," I murmured.

Aunt Gina always saw the best in us, despite our flaws.

"I hear you, but I'll be investing a lot of money into this. But I must admit that his plan does seem solid. I'm having someone at my office look over everything. I only gave him half of what he asked for and told him to come up with the rest. But even half was still a lot, especially given the fact that I've already helped him a few times, and nothing comes of it.

"What does Gable think of Brave's idea?"

I hesitated, feeling the weight of her question resting on my chest this time. I really didn't want to lie. "He...um…"

My phone lit up. Aurora was calling. "Uh, Auntie, let me call you back. I have to take this call," I said hurriedly.

"OK, honey. We'll talk later. I love you."

"I love you too, and tell Unc I said I hope he feels better soon."

"Will do. Bye now."

Relieved, I swiped to answer the call.

"Hello, Miss Turks and Caicos."

"Heyyy, B," she responded with a giggle.

"What's good? How was your trip?"

"It was amazing. I had the best time for the most part. I'll tell you all about it later when I come help you pack for our trip to DC."

I rolled my eyes. "I don't need help packing. And, honestly, you and Neveah have your own lives. Y'all don't need to babysit me. I'm truly grateful for y'all, but Ro, you have a six-year-old and a husband who needs your attention."

"Girl, who said you *needed* help?" she replied. "I'm coming over to help anyway. I appreciate your thoughtfulness, but Anderson and your niece will be fine. Plus, we need some space. He got on my nerve the last part of the trip, and he is still on it."

"Oh. Is everything okay between y'all?" I asked.

"Yeah, I guess." She sighed. "I don't know. Mostly it's good but when we argue, we really argue. It has gotten ugly a few times lately—like, ugly, ugly. It's kinda scary. I don't want my marriage to turn into my parents' marriage. Their arguing got so unbearable that I started to hate being home. I don't want that for Layla."

"Mm. That's not like y'all."

"Nope. I don't know what's up with him lately. Anyway, I'm coming over, and I'm bringing sushi. And wine."

I knew I wouldn't be drinking any wine, but I responded in agreement anyway. "Ok. I have some work to finish though. What time will you be here?"

"About five, after I pick Layla up from school and spend a couple of hours with her."

"OK. Ro. See you then."

I ended the call and exhaled. There was no need to fight with her or Neveah about being here for me. There was no winning. Those two wouldn't have it any other way.

I stood and did a few neck and leg stretches to release the stiffness of sitting too long, then settled back into my chair. I opened one of the files in front of me and scanned through it. A few documents I needed for the deposition were missing.

I texted Fallon a to-do list, which included gathering those missing documents. Slumping back in my chair, I texted Gabriella.

Me: *Hi, Gabriella. Have you heard from Gable? I found a safe in his office.*

I erased the second sentence before pressing send. I wasn't sure if I should mention the safe. I didn't know if I wanted Gable to know I found it before I knew what was in it.

Phone in hand, I left my office and went over to Gable's. I needed to try to get into this safe.

I sat on the recliner tucked in the corner and glanced around, carefully scanning every inch of the office, thinking.

"I could contact a locksmith," I mumbled.

I texted Neveah.

Me: *I could contact à locksmith.*

She replied almost instantly: *You could. Are you sure you're ready to know what's in those desk drawers and safe though?*

I frowned at the text.

Me: *Why wouldn't I want to know?*

Neveah: *I'm just saying, sis. May be a lot to handle. But whatever you decide, you know I got you.*

I let out a long grunt. I hadn't thought about what might be in there and how I might feel about its contents. I just knew something was there that Gable didn't want me to see. Confusion twisted around my neck muscles, tightening its grip. Tension climbed up the back of my head and settled behind my temples. Dropping the phone in my lap, I placed two fingers on both sides of my head and caressed, attempting to massage away the throbbing. *What am I going to do?*

A chime from my phone drew me from my thoughts, saving me from a spiral.

A text reply from Gabriella.

Gabriella: *He said you should receive a letter today. Not sure if you have gotten it yet.*

I headed to the mailbox, assuming the letter would have been mailed.

I always appreciated that my mailman ran early, before noon on most days.

I walked out to the mailbox and pulled the flap down. I pulled the mail out and desperately searched through the stack. Nothing.

Sighing. I walked back up my driveway toward the front door. My heart skipped a beat when I heard a vehicle. I turned to see a third-party delivery service van stopping in front of my house. I walked back to the end of the driveway, meeting the uniformed driver.

"Good afternoon, ma'am." He nods his head, handing me a manila envelope.

"Thank you. I responded, taking the envelope from him. It was addressed to me. No return address. Clever. He must have used a re-mailing service to avoid revealing the state he was in. The ridiculous lengths this man is going to hide his location lit a spark of anger in me.

Tearing the envelope open, I hurried back inside. Pulling the letter out, I rushed to my room, plopped down on the chaise and read.

Hey There, One True Love of My Life.

I miss you so much. I'm sorry for putting you through all of this, but trust

me when I say, I have your best interest at heart. Gabriella told me she met with you on Saturday morning. After she told me about how upset you were, I knew I had to overnight this letter to you, ASAP. I understand your frustration. Being away from you, it's killing me—no pun intended—that I am going through this

too. I know you are searching for answers, but I think the less you know, the better for you. I know you, Blou. The more you know, the more you'll try to fix this, to change my mind and hold it all together for both of us. I can't let you do that.

I will tell you that I have started treatment. I should start to see how the illness reacts to the medication within the week. One of the reasons I don't want you to see me is because it's strong dose of medication that can have a harsh effect on my body. The less you see me go through the more you can remember me as strong and healthy. If I do not recover from this, I don't want your happy memories of me to be replaced with sad and traumatizing experiences. But, I am praying that I will recover. I am hopeful that I'll return home to you—maybe in two or three months, maybe six. Since this is a new medication that is being tested on an aggressive illness, they can't be entirely sure of anything. That's the downside of being used as a test dummy, I guess.

Gabriella told me about the panic attack. I'm so sorry, Blou.

It's been so long since you've had one. It pains me to know that I'm the cause. But I fear you would suffer more if you had to watch me go through this. To take care of me or worse, watching me deteriorate would add another layer to your anxiety, intensifying it.

I've been talking to a therapist since I found out about the illness and have continued to talk to him virtually after my arrival here. My doctor recommended it to help me process all of this. I'm glad I did. It's helped tremendously.

When I left you the first letter, I meant what I told you about moving on if this is too much for you. I mean it when I say I have your best interest at heart. Even if it means losing you, I want you to be happy. I know this is hard, but please do whatever will make you the happiest. Give yourself permission to let go if you need to.

I will write again soon.

I love you deeply,

Gable

I closed my eyes. More apologies, and still not enough answers.

A guttural cry rose from deep in the pit of my stomach and pierced my throat. Clutching the letter tightly in trembling hands, I watched the words blur as tears flooded my eyes.

Gable might think he was doing this for me, but this felt a lot like torture, not love. Defeat tied me in a knot that I could no longer stomach.

I bolted to the bathroom just in time, collapsing over the toilet as I regurgitated this morning's coffee.

I pulled myself up. I needed to pull myself together—a shower, some fresh air, and food to bring some kind of normalcy to my life. Some calmness.

After I showered, I thew on a soft floral short set, grabbed my tote, and a water bottle and headed for the garage.

As the garage door creaked up, I remembered the card Gabriella had given me for the therapist. I opened the center console, took out the card, and looked it over again.

What can it hurt? I thought.

I pulled my phone from the tote and dialed the number.

"Dr. Butler's office. How may I help you?"

I froze, rethinking my decision.

"Hello?"

"Um…Hi. I'm calling to schedule an appointment with Dr. Butler please."

"Sure. Will you be a new client?"

"Um. Yes." Nervousness crept into my fingers. My hands shook lightly as I held on to the card.

"OK. Great. I just need to gather a few details from you, and we can get you scheduled."

After a series of questions, the appointment was set. I backed out of the driveway with no clue of my destination. Suddenly, I became intensely aware of the hunger that had manifested in my stomach—an aching emptiness.

After driving for about fifteen minutes, I settled on my favorite seafood restaurant, Lauren's, nestled off in the cut on the waterfront.

When I arrived, the hostess seated me outside, upon my request. I ordered my usual salmon salad. While waiting, I pulled out my phone and searched for a locksmith.

As I searched, I pondered on Neveah's advice. She wasn't wrong, but I needed to do this. I would just have to prepare myself for what I might find.

I went down the list calling locksmiths until I came across one who had a technician available to come to the house this evening. All I needed to show was identification and documentation showing that I owned the property where the safe was located. How perfect.

The waitress placed my salad on the table just as I ended the call with the locksmith. I eyed the salad as my stomach let out a low rumble. I don't think I had had this kind of appetite since before I read the first *Dear Jane* letter from Gable.

I still had so much to process, so many decisions to make. I didn't even know where to start.

I took a bite of my salad. My eyes drifted, admiring the beautiful ocean, its color a mix of blue and green. The South Florida beaches were one of the reasons I'd decided to move back home after college. I loved the breathtaking waters. The aqua hue made it that much more delightful to be here.

My thoughts sinking deeper into the lull of the ocean's waves, I wondered if it might be easier to walk away from Gable than it was to go through all of this. The way he was handling this situation made me doubt that things would ever be the same between us...if he survived this.

Eating alone brought back a pleasant memory of when Gable and I first met right after I moved back to Parksdale.

Still heartbroken over Zamir, one night, I'd decided to take myself out to a nice dinner. I got dressed up in a black dress that cinched my petite waist and hugged every curve of my hips and around my round derrière.

Leaving my car with the valet, I sashayed toward the front entrance of the restaurant. Just as I'd reached to open the door, it swung open from the inside. A guy was coming out. He stepped aside holding the door open for me, a smile touching his beautiful eyes. Slipping past him, I nodded and returned a slight smile.

"I have a reservation for one," I said to the young woman standing behind the maître d' station, dressed neatly in all-black attire.

"The name?" she asked with a polite smile.

"My name is Blou...Blou Rivers."

Another hostess walked up with one menu in her hand.

"Right this way, ma'am."

She led me to a cozy booth toward the back of the softly lit dining room. I sank into the seat, admiring the flickering candle on the table—the perfect ambience for a romantic dinner. Too bad

I'm dining alone, I thought.

Glancing around the immaculately designed dining room, I remembered when Zamir would take me to upscale venues in DC. He was into fine dining just as much as I was. I'd felt a weight of sadness settling on my shoulders. I thought a nice night out alone would help me get my mind off him, but being at that restaurant really wasn't helping. Everything reminded me of him. He was the only man that I had ever loved. We'd shared so much of ourselves with each other during the four years we were exclusive. Our relationship was built on a friendship that I thought would last forever—a friendship that began in high school.

"Ma'am, can I get you a glass of wine?"

Knowing what I wanted without opening the menu, I answered, "Yes. Banshee, Sauvignon Blanc, and a bottle of San Pellegrino, please."

"Good choice. I'll get that for you." She smiled before turning on her heels and walking away.

Minutes later, she came back with a whole bottle of the wine I requested. "Oh, no. I—I only wanted a glass."

"Yes, but the gentlemen at the bar sent this over." She'd pointed discreetly.

I followed her gaze. It was the same guy who had held the door open for me. He waved and nodded. I blushed. A flood of heat rushed through my body. The waitress grinned wide as though the wine had been gifted to her. She walked away, leaving me fidgeting in my own bashfulness.

Not knowing what to do, where to look or what to think, I pulled out my phone to distract myself. A message from the group text with Neveah and Aurora lit up.

Neveah: *How's your solo date?*

I was just about to respond when a deep voice rang out from above me. "Dining alone?"

I slowly looked up, already bracing myself. And there he was, the beautiful creature from across the room. My heart thumped at the sight of him hovering over my table. I didn't know if I should be creeped out or flattered.

"Something like that," I uttered quietly, gazing into his almond-shaped, doe-brown eyes. He looked to be older than my twenty-five years, but he wore his age well. A wide grin spread across his face, revealing deep dimples that only deepened my attraction to him. He was devastatingly handsome. The cream-colored suit that complemented his body was cut perfectly in all the right places. I willed my face to remain unmoved, determined not to give away any hints of my body betraying me with a fierce desire at the sight of this gorgeous man.

"Would you like company?" he asked with hopeful eyes.

I hesitated. "Um…I—"

"I promise I'm not some crazy stalker. I was here for a business meeting. I saw you come in earlier. I couldn't leave without properly introducing myself to such a beautiful woman."

His smooth voice was soothing; his smile warm and inviting.

I sat back and crossed my arms, an amused smile dancing on my face. "Crazy stalkers always say they're not crazy stalkers, you know."

He chuckled. His laugh was infectious. I laughed too.

"Go ahead and have a seat, but don't think I won't scream bloody murder if I have to." I warned, half serious, half amused.

From the time he sat down across from me, we talked and laughed like we were old friends. Three hours of euphoric haze. For a while, all the heartache faded to the background. I felt free.

The nostalgic daydream dissolved, pulling me back to the present at the sound of the server's voice. "How are you doing over here, ma'am?" she asked.

"Fine. Thank you." I glanced at the time on my watch. I didn't have long before Aurora's and the locksmith's arrival. "I'm ready for the check, please."

Chapter *nine*

I was in my office reviewing the documents I'd requested from Fallon when the doorbell rang. I checked the camera app to see Aurora standing at the door holding a take-out bag. I pressed the microphone icon and spoke into the phone. "One second. I'll be right there."

As I opened the door to let her in, the locksmith van pulled into the driveway.

"Freddy's Locksmith?" Aurora squinted at the logo on the van, then she turned to me, her eyebrows drawn together. "You called a locksmith?"

I motioned her inside. "Yes. I'll fill you in."

I waited at the door as the locksmith approached.

"Blou Rivers-Whitmore?"

I nodded. I felt a pinch of embarrassment. I shouldn't need someone to open anything in my own house.

"Hi. I am Clint with Freddy's Locksmith." He extended a hand. I shook it.

"Come on in." I said, turning toward the foyer.

"I have an order to open a safe. I'll need to see your photo ID and proof of residency."

Aurora had placed the bag on the kitchen counter and returned to the foyer. She leaned casually against the wall with her arms crossed over her chest, listening intently, curiosity radiating from her.

I grabbed my ID and mortgage deed from the table near the entryway and handed it to him.

He examined both and handed them back.

"Looks good. Lead the way," he said with a slight smile.

Both he and Aurora followed as I moved through the house, leading us to Gable's office. I opened the cabinet door, exposing the safe.

"Here ya go."

"Good deal," he said, crouching in front of it. "Should only take a couple minutes."

"You want to tell me what this is about?" Aurora whispered, her eyes wide.

"I will. Chill," I whispered back.

As Clint worked, I sucked in a deep breath. With each passing second, the weight of not knowing what I was about to find in that safe sat heavier on my chest. I glanced at Aurora, her attention fixed on me. A wave of relief passed over me. I was happy that I wasn't alone.

"I have no idea what I'm about to find in that safe," I whispered to her.

She drew in a deep breath, filling her cheeks with air, then slowly released it. Threading her arms around mine, she whispered back, "I don't know what's happening right now, but whatever you find—if you find anything—I got you, sis."

"All done." Clint rose from the floor and turned to face us.

"Thank you," I said, managing a faint smile. "Oh, I forgot to ask when I called: Are you able to unlock these desk drawers as well?

He glanced at the desk, then back at me, then glanced at the desk again.

"Mm. Sure," he answered, his eyes filled with questions he would not dare ask. "I can add it to the invoice."

"Great," I replied.

After the desk drawers were unlocked, I paid and walked him to the front door, leaving Aurora in the office.

My heart's pace increased with every step I took back toward the office.

Aurora had taken a seat in the corner chair.

"What in the world is going on, B?" She sat up straight but remained seated.

I filled her in on the letters, my meeting with Gabriella, the locked drawers and finding the safe.

She stood and wrapped her arms around me in a tight embrace. "B, I'm so sorry. This is all...a lot."

"I know." Tears slipped from the corners of my eyes. "And I don't know what I am about to find." I stared at the safe.

"You know what you need to do?" she asked, taking both my hands into hers.

"What?" I cocked my head, curious.

"Pray. We need to pray."

"Mm. OK." Though I am a Christian, prayer was the one thing I did not do enough of, but I was doing a lot better lately. She was right. That is the one thing I didn't do after finding this safe.

She had been my prayer partner since middle school. Even when prayer wasn't my first instinct in the middle of a crisis, it was always hers.

Though she now attended a non-denominational church, she had grown up southern Baptist. As for Neveah and I, our families had always opted for non-denominational congregations.

I squeezed her hand and closed my eyes as she prayed aloud. I silently prayed for guidance and peace of mind, no matter what I found hidden away.

After the Amen, I opened my eyes, dropped Aurora's hand, and stepped toward the desk.

I didn't know where to start—the drawers, or the safe.

I stared at the open safe before slowly walking toward it and sitting down in front of it.

Aurora stayed seated in the corner chair. I sensed she wanted to give me space.

Inside sat a manila envelope and a small wooden box with a combination lock. I winced. *Not another lock.*

I pulled out the manila envelope and cracked it open, peeking inside. There were photos inside. My stomach was fluttering, queasiness blossoming. I slowly eased them out.

"Ro," I called out barely above a whisper.
She was by my side in seconds. "What is it?" she asked gently, kneeling beside me. Together, we stared at the images in my hand.

"Girl…whose baby is that?" She was giving voice to exactly what I was thinking.

I shrugged. Tears welled up again as my mind wondered in every possible direction.

Aurora slid the photo from my fingers and flipped it over. "There's a date on the back. No name."

I looked at her, silently pleading for answers I knew she did not have.

"It's dated 2018." She reached for other photos scattered in front of me and checked the back of them. Each was a photo of the same child. Each with a different year scribbled on the back: 2018, 2019, 2020, 2021, 2022, 2023, 2024. Seven photos of a growing boy.

The room felt like it was closing in. I sat frozen. A wave of shock slammed into me, knocking the breath from my lungs. I closed my eyes, trying to remain calm but the tremble that rolled through my body warned me that this was too much too soon.

Shaking my head, I quickly gathered all the pictures. "I can't do this." I stuffed them back into the envelope, tossed it into the safe and slammed it shut. I wasn't concerned about it locking. Clint had deactivated the code.

As I stood, Aurora stood too, concern piercing through her eyes as she watched my every move.

"I can't do this," I repeated, voice sharper now. "Let's just get out of here. I need some air."

And with that, I stormed from the office, leaving behind the desk drawers, the safe and Gable's secrets.

Chapter *ten*

On the two-and-a-half-hour flight to DC, I had hoped to get some sleep, but even the low hum of the plane couldn't lull me into a steady nap. I'd spent the past few nights tossing and turning, nightmares and ruminating thoughts invading my rest.

I had decided not to go back into Gable's office until after my therapy appointment on Monday. I figured it would be best to talk through what I had already uncovered before opening Pandora's box again.

I couldn't get the little handsome face in those photos out of my mind. The small boy bore an undeniable resemblance to Gable. There was no way this little boy was not his son. But how…why, did Gable keep this from me?

The picture of the boy when he was a newborn was dated 2018, but it didn't have a month. Gable and I became official in February of 2018. Was he cheating on me? There was no way I could have ever imagined this.

I slid the cover to the window seat open and stared into the clouds, drifting back to the first conversation Gable and I had about starting a family.

It was the day after Valentines Day. I sat on the bed reading,

Gable lying beside me. We hadn't gone out, just stayed in watching movies, talking, playing cards, and making love. It had been two months since the day we'd met at the restaurant.

"I want us to be official," he'd said, pulling me out of the book.

Closing it, I turned to face him, confused. "What? Aren't we already?"

"We never talked about it."

"I mean, I've been seeing only you since December. We spend all our time together, and you practically live here. I figured we already were."

He took my hands. "Yes, we have been inseparable, but we never said we were exclusive."

"Oookay," I rolled my eyes, shaking my head. "We're official then."

"What? Are you upset?"

"No. It's just, some things go without saying. I thought what's between us was already understood." I caught his eyes with mine. We locked into each other's stare.

Breaking his gaze, he slides his eyes to our hands. "But I want more," he'd said, looking back at me. "I want us to get married."

I froze. "What? I…We…" I struggled to find words. His confession caught me completely off guard. "Gable, it's only been two months." And according to you, we just started 'officially' dating two seconds ago," I said, sarcastically, pumping air quotes at *officially*.

"I know, but it feels like years and I'm not getting any younger." His eyes searched mine, silently pleading.

"You're only five years older than me and we're both still pretty young. What's the rush?"

I caught a brief sparkle in his eyes at that question.

"Gable, I…" I took a breath, pausing to choose my next words carefully. "You know I don't want children. I know you do."

His jaws tightened. He'd looked away, but his grip on my hands grew stronger. The silence between us seemed to linger for eternity.

Then, his eyes locked back on mine. "Blou, you are the most

important person in my life. I choose you over anything and any-one. Since I have known you, life without you doesn't make sense. Marry me. I'll choose you always, every day, no matter what. I promise."

My gaze didn't waver and neither did his. I'd leaned in, resting my forehead gently against his.

"I love you so much. I want forever with you too, babe, but I'm one hundred percent sure I don't ever plan to have children. I need you to be certain that you're okay with that."

With an unpredictable, swift launch forward, he swept me up and laid me on my back, covering my body with his. Pressing against me, his erection growing, he'd planted soft kisses on my neck, gentling sucking my skin. I'd moaned, succumbing to all that he wanted from me.

Finding my face, his eyes bore into mine, lighting a wild flame deep within my soul.

"I want you, no matter what." His voice was hushed and rasping, each word catching in his throat as if he'd do anything to wrap them around me, binding me to him forever.

With slow, soft kisses, he'd eased down, his lips meeting my breasts, gripping each one as he tenderly massaged, sucked, and kissed every inch of them. Reaching down between my legs, searching for the treasure that he longed for, his fingers had found me shamelessly pulsating and wet with desire, signaling to him that I was ready and aching to feel all of him. I moaned as he'd filled me inch by inch with his eager hardness.

His eyes found mine, locking them in place, his steady pace deliberate and measured with each stroke. "Blou, will you be my wife?" Lowering his face he gently brushed his lips against the curve of my neck. "Please." His gentle plea tickled warmly against my skin.

My hips swayed in sync with his motion. The ebb and flow of our rhythm sent us both into an orgasmic frenzy, as our bodies trembled with pleasure.

"Yes," I moaned. "I will be your wife."

"Forever?" He whispered, lips pressing against my ear.

"Forever," I whispered back.

We landed in DC early in the evening but decided to stay in. Room service, cozy pajamas, and the safety of our sister circle were just the reprieve the three of us needed. Over comfort food, wine, playlists, and a change of scenery, we begin to unwind— emptying our overflowing cups of the week's messiness, hoping to refill them with something gentler, nourishment for our hearts and minds.

We laughed and reminisced about our college days, swapped grievances and tallied the few pleasures we were holding on to in our day-to-day lives. My pleasure list was short. Gable had made sure of that. Hiding an illness from me and disappearing had been more than enough. But after finding the contents of the safe, I couldn't shake this eerie feeling that the deeper I dug, the more I'd uncover a mountain of deception. I kept wondering if our entire life together had been a facade.

I wanted to focus on anything other than that for the rest of the trip, so, grasping for something to talk about other than Gable's sordid secrets, I shared the details of my meet-up with Brave.

"Girl, I don't know about that," Aurora said, raising an eyebrow. "I love Brave like he's my own little brother, but trusting him with an investment? *Um.*"

Neveah shook her head. "I think it's a great way for them to bond, and besides, this gives him the opportunity to build trust," she countered.

"They can bond by going to the movies, over dinner, or even by talking, which is something they rarely do, by the way, but investments? *Nah,*" Aurora scoffed.

Neveah rolled her eyes.

"Must y'all always go at it?" I interjected before the back-and-forth turned into a full-blown debate, as usual.

"I'm just saying," Neveah shrugged, "I believe in Brave. He's only twenty-two, but he's maturing. Sure, he has had to learn some hard lessons. That's a part of life. He's growing. I think this time will be different."

"I just hope you're right," I said, even though I wasn't sure if I was making the best decision.

"I am," Neveah said, tossing a pillow at me. "Now go pop some popcorn so we can binge watch Sweet Magnolias until we fall asleep."

I laughed. "Three bags of buttery popcorn coming right up."

Surprisingly, sleep found me with ease and I woke up feeling more rested than I had in days. I don't know if I was so tired that my body couldn't resist or if the comfort of having my girls with me in a different atmosphere soothed me into a rare peace that had been too difficult to find lately.

As I soaked in a long, hot bath before it was time to dress for the evening's mix and mingle, I basked in the fullness of the day. We had spent the day drifting between the spa, shopping, and our favorite dining spots that we discovered during our college days.

Being back here felt nostalgic. As we wandered the city earlier, memories of me and Zamir surfaced—late nights on campus, cruising all over the DMV, and our frequent spontaneous road trips to New York, Jersey, and Philly.

I'd applied to Howard for two reasons: Their strong law program and because it was an HBCU. My dad and I talked a lot about college before he passed. He supported my decision, although he preferred that I attend Harvard, his and my mom's alma mater. He was a real estate attorney, so my choice to study law made him even prouder.

Since I was seven, I'd known the love story of how they were high school sweethearts turned college and life-long soulmates. Every year on their wedding anniversary, I listened with amusement as they retold their two slightly different versions with a loving clash.

After my mom died, my dad carried the story alone. As I got older, he shared stories of their college days that I hadn't heard before, speaking of her with admiration in his voice and an unadulterated love in his eyes. Painting pictures of the past with laughter and reverence, he reminisced, taking me on a trip with him down memory lane every chance he had.

After my father became very ill, he made me promise him I would go where my heart led me, that my college experience would be well lived and that whenever I met the love of my life, I wouldn't let anything, or anyone come between us.

So, when Zamir and I decided to break up five months after our college graduation, I wrestled with the decision. We'd spent the last six years furthering our education at Howard. I earned my bachelor's degree and then completed law school while he simultaneously completed a bachelor's degree and then a master's degree. During the last four years of college, we dated exclusively, falling deeper in love.

Our breakup felt like a betrayal of that promise to my father. At the time, I felt with all my heart that Zamir was the love of my life, that he was my future and my forever. But staying together felt too much like forcing ourselves to maintain a difficult long-distance relationship with no clear end in sight.

My mind wandered, deeper into a hole of vulnerability. I thought back to the final conversation that ended us.

"This is an opportunity of a lifetime," Zamir had said, excited about his job offer. "Not many students get offered a position like this fresh out of college." He grinned.

"That's good news, babe." I smiled though it didn't quite reach my eyes. I tried my best to be happy for him.

"We can build the life we always talked about right here in DC or New York," he said, gently taking both my hands into his, "since I will be back-and-forth between the offices."

I tilted my head, meeting his gaze. "Zamir, babe, I'm not staying here. You know I've always planned to go back home after college."

His eyes, lit with excitement just a moment ago, had dimmed.

"Since you don't have a job at a firm there yet, and I have a job here, I was thinking, maybe you can look at firms here."

The gentle squeeze of his hands sent warmth through my body, tugging at the strings of my heart. His touch had always had that effect on me.

I slowly shook my head. "I can't. I have to go back home. My mom and dad, they—" I paused, "Their graves are there. All the memories I have with them are in Parksdale."

I searched his eyes for understanding. The walls in the tight space of his bedroom seemed to close in around us. The weight of the silence pressed against our suddenly fragile relationship.

He swallowed hard, his eyes laced with sadness and empathy. He nodded. "I understand."

Looking away, he released my hands and turned away. The bed shifted beneath me as the weight of his six-foot solid frame unburdened the mattress when he stood, leaving me to sit in the encumbrance of our decisions.

Sharp pangs of emotional heaviness had settled deep in my stomach. *I understand.* That's it. The ache of rejection stole my ability to speak.

My tear-filled eyes followed him as he walked over to the mini fridge on the opposite side of the room. He pulled out two bottles of water.

Turning to face me, he hesitated before moving back toward me. His misty eyes met mine. The pain he held in his steady glance echoed the hollow burn inside of me.

Handing me the bottle of water, he lowered to his knees in front of me.

"Blou, I—" A tear streamed down his face. I gently slid my trembling thumb over his cheek wiping the single tear, wishing it was just as easy to wipe away our sorrows.

A sacred pause filled the space between us as we stared into each other's eyes. We leaned in, our mouths crashing together hungrily.

Pulling back slightly he moaned, "I love you, Blou." His teeth lightly biting my bottom lip.

Sliding his arms around my waist, he lowered his head and rested it on my lap. "I don't want to lose you baby," he said quietly, a soft ache dripping from his voice, "but I'll never stand in the way of you doing what's best for you."

My heart quickened, thumping fiercely against my chest. Releasing my waist, he straightened. Our eyes tangled in the midst of the quiet storm.

I nodded. A silent understanding passed between us. Sitting down next to me, he pulled me close. Neither of us wanted to say what our wet faces and dancing heartbeats concluded. We clung to each other, chest to chest, our faces buried in the curves of the other's neck.

Pulling back, I wiped my face with the back of my hand. "I'll be here until my lease is up," I said, barely audible. "What do you want to do until then?"

He lowered his face into his hands, slowly shaking his head. "I can't," he said, in a hushed tone. "I can't think about that right now."

He lifted his head but looked away, his gaze fixed on the wall in front of us. "I'm sorry." His voice cracked under the strain. "I need some time."

Tension thickened the air. His words landed like a blow to my already nauseated gut.

"OK," I whispered, training my vision toward my own spot on the wall.

Saddled with the grief of our unspoken truth, I forced myself off the bed, quickly stuffed the pieces of clothing I had scattered around Zamir's room into my Brandon Blackwood backpack, slipped on my sneakers, and moved toward the door.

Twisting the doorknob, I turned back hoping to see Zamir coming toward me.

He sat quietly on the bed. His mind was made up and so was mine.

"See you later," I muttered, just loud enough for my words to reach him.

His gaze swept across my face, then drifted back to the wall.

"See you later," he said softly, almost reluctantly, sucking the breath out of me with his words. We both knew that both our hesitant, *see you laters,* were fancy disguises for final goodbyes.

I rushed through his apartment and out the door, not stopping until I reached my car.

Once inside, I came completely undone, every seam of my body had split wide open under the weight of the emotional pressure flooding my aching heart.

I cried every day for a week before deciding that life didn't stop because someone left me—again.

When Zamir didn't come after me that day, I convinced myself that our relationship was for a season and that season was over. Leaving was not in his plans and staying was not in mine. Staying would have only been for him. Zamir meant the world to me, but I couldn't see myself making that decision unless we were at least engaged. And he didn't ask me to marry him.

When the topic came up before, he'd candidly expressed he wasn't ready for marriage, that he wanted to start his career before taking on that kind of responsibility. It tore my soul to hear that from the man I loved so deeply, but I knew he was right. Sometimes love was not enough to close the distance between two paths winding along in opposite directions.

Not long after Zamir and I broke up, I was offered a position with Jones & Jones as a family law attorney. It was early December when I packed up and left DC to settle back into my hometown, joining Aurora and Neveah who had left two months prior.

The break-up was one of the hardest things I'd endured, second only to losing my parents. Zamir wanted to remain friends; I knew that would be too hard for me. I cut off all communication completely.

He'd called for several weeks before giving up. The sight of his name pricked something soft inside me each time it lit up my screen, but I refused to block his number. Still, I let every call go to voicemail. He left a message each time.

Each message was like a sealed letter that I could never bring myself to open. I feared I would shatter if I heard him say goodbye again. But deleting them would bring a finality that I wasn't ready for, so I tucked each one away in my storage cloud, unheard and untouched, even now.

Dressed in cocktail dresses and stilettos, my besties and I stepped inside of the venue fashionably late, an hour after the event's start time.

The medium-sized space was nicely decked out in the school's colors, the DJ was spinning old school jams, while bodies on the dance floor gyrated, two-stepped, crip walked, and however else the music swayed them. The air was saturated with the mingling scents of woody and spicy colognes and sweet and flowery perfumes.

"Let's grab this table over there." Aurora leaned in so we could hear her over the music.

Following her lead, I scanned the room for familiar faces. Between the dim lighting and the fact that I hadn't seen many people from my class in person since graduation, I didn't recognize anyone. I only kept in contact with a hand full of college classmates online, unlike Neveah, who followed half the class on social media.

"Girl, there's Bret Davis." Neveah tugged on my arm and pointed to a guy standing by the DJ's booth. "I'll be right back, I'm gonna say hello."

"You haven't talked to that man since college…right?" I frowned.

She rolled her eyes. "No, I haven't, but that's the point of a mix and mingle, babe. You mix and you mingle. Loosen up. Have fun." She sauntered off.

Neveah was a social butterfly. She'd have a conversation with almost every person in this room and exchange phone numbers with a few before the night was over. I, on the other hand, preferred keeping conversations to a strict minimum.

"*Ohhhh*. This is my jam," Aurora shrieked. "Come on. Let's dance."

She grabbed my hand.

"Um. I'm good. You go ahead," I said, slowly pulling my hand back and taking a seat at the table.

She paused, giving me a look that was half concern, half disappointment. For a second, I thought she'd push, but instead, she nodded and gave an understanding smile. Bouncing to the music, her burnt orange micro locs swayed as she moved toward the dance floor, as Mary J's "Just Fine" pumped through the speakers.

I smiled and shook my head at my friend. She was our hype woman. At every party we'd been to over the years she was the life of it. She could always be found on the dance floor moving rhythmically to whatever beat that was blasting while egging everyone on, whether they could dance or not.

Tuning everyone out, I sat, admiring the centerpiece on the table. Grabbing a mint from a small glass dish, I unwrapped it and popped it into my mouth. As the DJ switched tracks, I felt myself slightly rocking to the music.

"Blou Rivers?"

I looked up into the face of Monica Low. Her last name described her perfectly, except it was missing the down and dirty. She stood over me with a wide grin plastered across her face.

"Girl, I haven't seen you in forever," she screeched. I was sure my facial expression revealed that I was not as excited to see her as she pretended she was to see me. In fact, I wasn't thrilled at all.

In college, this woman had relentlessly flirted with Zamir every chance she got. I still remembered the time she'd tried to follow him into the bathroom at a frat party. Then, later she claimed amnesia, blaming it on too much alcohol and asking if I'd like to come to a girl's night with her and her friends. After declining her offer, she made it a point to tell me how Zamir was too good for me and she didn't see what he saw in me.

"Hey," I mumbled, struggling to keep my face from twisting.

Uninvited, she took a seat in the chair next to me and placed her drink on the table. She hadn't aged well. The crow's feet around her tired eyes made her look ten years older. The full, stiff bobbed wig, and even bang across the forehead, might have added a few more years to her small face. I was in no position to cast stones, but she looked like life had been raking her over for some time now.

"You look good, girl—better than I thought you would. I thought by now you would have had a house full of babies from your college sweetie." Dropping her voice just above a whisper, she leaned in. "And you know what having all those babies does to our bodies." She giggled.

I glared as she picked up her drink and gulped down the rest of the contents of the glass.

She placed the glass back on the table and continued her tiresome prattling.

"So…" She paused, leaned in even closer, and in normal Monica Low's fashion, rambled on and on. "A little birdie told me that Zamir got married—but to someone other than you. Girl, I was so sorry to hear that. I never thought y'all would ever break up. I always loved y'all together. I haven't been able to find you on social media anywhere, but I heard that you tied the knot real fast after that. No judgement. Nothing wrong with a rebound."

She gave my hand a quick pat, her eyes flicking to my wedding ring. "That's a beautiful ring, girl. Speaking of husbands and rebounds, where is yours? Is he here?" She smirked.

I wanted to knock that smug look right off her face. I bit my bottom lip to keep from saying exactly what I was thinking. My icy glare must have spoken for me, though, because she straightened abruptly and stood, grabbing her empty glass.

"OK, girl. It was nice chatting with you. I need to visit the ladies' room," she said and stumbled off.

I rolled my eyes. Classic Monica. It was no surprise to me that Ms. Low Down was already tipsy, less than two hours into the party. Back in college, she drank too much too fast and couldn't hold her liquor to save her life.

With my college thorn in the side gone to find someone else to piss off, I let myself relax a little. But her words lingered: *rebound.*

I never considered Gable a rebound. But what if Monica was right? I married him because I loved him—really loved him. Still, I couldn't deny that I still loved Zamir when Gable and I married. I knew I could never have the life with Zamir that I desperately wished for, so I moved on instead of dwelling on what could have been. I should have known better than to let anything a quidnunc like Monica said get to me. But it did.

I fidgeted with my ring, turning it on my finger. A sadness shadowed my mood as I thought about Gable not being here. The sadness was quickly replaced by a cycle of emotions—anger, disappointment, and fear wrapped around me, squeezing my chest, every ounce of extroverted energy I had left dissipating, and I just wanted to hide between the walls of my home. My face flushed with heat. My breath shortened. Trembles followed.

No, no, no. Not here. My thoughts raced just as quickly as my heart.

I pushed from the chair and made a beeline toward the door leading outside. The burst of fresh air hit my face releasing a wave of relief. I leaned against the brick building, closed my eyes and steadied my breathing. I could feel the tightness in my chest releasing its hold.

"Too much in there for you, huh?"

I froze.

I slowly opened my eyes. A surge radiated my entire body at the sight of the man standing in front of me. I was at a loss for words as I stared at him as he studied me.

He stepped closer and took my hand with familiar ease, his finger lightly brushing over my wedding ring.

"Are you OK?" he asked.

I stole a glance at our hands and then found his eyes again. "Um…um…yeah." I nodded my head, slowly slipping my hand from his gentle grip.

My eyes raked over his tall frame, admiring how his toned build perfectly filled the fitted tee and tailored blazer. His deep cocoa skin still just as smooth and beautiful as I remembered it. Warm dark brown eyes drew me in and held me there. Pulling my bottom lip in between my teeth, I inhaled deeply, trying to steady my rapid heart—now racing for a different reason.

"Wow. It's been so long, he said, a soft smile curling his lips. "How have you been?"

"I've been good," I managed. "What about you?"

He shrugged. "Life is life. I've been OK." Something flickered in his eyes, a hint of sadness, maybe.

"Are you still living in Florida?" he asked, his eyes never leaving mine.

My gaze slipped free for a moment. "Yeah," I said quietly, searching his handsome face. He'd aged well—he looked almost the same. Now he wore a goatee, different from when he only wore a thin mustache in

college. "I see you're still here—just like you said you'd be." I blinked.

Tears burned behind my eyes. I looked away, refusing to let them fall. The emotions welling up inside of me were nothing I would have imagined feeling if I ever saw him again.

He tilted his head. "Well, actually I—"

"OMG! If it isn't *the* Zamir Collins!" Neveah's voice rang out as she came rushing up, Aurora right behind her.

"Hey, there." He pulled them into a quick group hug. Pulling back, he grinned at them.

"Hey, bro!" Aurora grinned back, her eyes cutting toward me.

Neveah stepped to my side. "I've been looking all over for you. You good?" She searched my face for answers.

I forced a smile. "Yeah, I'm fine. Let's go back inside." I gave Zamir a quick glance before stepping past him.

"You coming inside?" I heard Aurora ask Zamir behind me. I turned back toward them, waiting for his answer.

"No. I was about to head out. I have an early flight in the morning." Our eyes met briefly before I turned away. "Blou."

His hand wrapped softly around my wrist. I turned, my heart leaped.

"It was nice seeing you," he whispered, fragile and slow. "I wish we had more time to catch up."

A gentle smile I hadn't expected eased across my face. "You too," I said, ignoring the latter. I slipped my wrist from his hand, and without looking back, I walked into the venue—praying the rest of the night would go smoothly and fast.

Chapter *eleven*

I stared out of my office window. After a week off, I still wasn't sure I was ready to return, but duty called. And if having Gable constantly on my mind wasn't enough, I couldn't seem to shake my encounter with Zamir either.

I was so confused by the overwhelming emotional flood that washed over me when I saw him that I didn't even mention it to the girls. I needed a moment of introspection before welcoming anyone else's opinions, especially knowing Neveah and Aurora's would vastly differ. It was rare that they agreed on anything.

My body's visceral reaction to seeing Zamir was so raw. It should have felt wrong, but for some reason our connection still felt pure and electrifying. It felt right, but it was so wrong. My husband might be MIA but I was still very married. It was probably just the D.C. vibe, the nostalgia. Nothing more.

I didn't know exactly what Gable was hiding. I suspected that whatever it was, it was going to change our lives forever. Our lives had already been greatly altered with this illness, and with him leaving. I kept going back and forth in my head and heart, trying to make sense of all of it. I didn't even know if I believed he was really sick.

Finding the safe and the pictures of the little boy manifested doubt and mistrust, something I had never felt before with Gable. For all I knew, he could be with the mother of that child right now, but I know nothing for sure, which was why I needed to go back into his office to see what else I could piece together. I planned to as soon as I got home.

Gable's disappearance and secrets were unsettling. They had me on edge for days. But Zamir's presence came laced with calmness, lighting me up in a way that I didn't know was still possible.

The day I meant Zamir was still so vivid in my mind. It was the summer before our senior year in high school. Neveah, Aurora and I, were at the movies in line about to purchase tickets to a matinee. I had opened my purse to pull out my wallet when it fell, spilling most of its contents. Embarrassed, I'd quickly stooped down to gather my belongings.

"Need some help?"

I looked up into the most handsome face I'd ever seen, wearing a perfect set of thick dark eyebrows, over the most gorgeous dark brown eyes. A curly temp fade enhanced his slim brown face.

As he kneeled beside me, his eyes steadied on mine. I smiled sheepishly, stumbling over my words.

"I…*um*…No. I got it. Thank you," I said, stuffing my things back into my purse.

He picked up my school ID, glancing over it. A wide grin spread across his face. "Oh, you go to Parksdale High School. Cool. I'll be starting there this upcoming school year. I'm going to be a senior."

"Yes. I go there. Did you just move here? Easing my ID from his hand, I straightened, standing to my feet. He followed, standing tall over me.

"Yes. Kinda. I mean, I've been coming here for summers with my dad but I'll be staying this time."

"Oh, OK." I didn't know if that was good or bad. I searched his face for something that might give away how he felt about moving. Questions filled my head, but it wasn't my place to ask a stranger about his personal business.

"Girl, you are holding up the line," Aurora snapped.

I turned to see that they had already purchased their tickets and had moved out of the line. Neveah was wearing a silly grin and Aurora stood with her arms crossed over her chest, half-amused, half-annoyed.

"Oh…I…I have to go."

"OK. Nice meeting you, Blou Rivers. I hope to see you around."

I frowned, then remembered he must have gotten my name from my ID.

He gave me a coy smile before turning and walking away. I smiled to myself as I slipped my student ID and a five-dollar bill under the window in exchange for my matinee ticket. The smile faded when I realized I didn't get his name.

Pulling myself from old memories, I took a sip of cold coffee from my *Best Attorney Ever* mug, which Aunt Gina had gifted me for Christmas.

I don't know if seeing Zamir was good timing or terrible timing but for now, I needed to refocus—to pick up the pieces of my life that have so suddenly shattered. Besides, that was one encounter in several years, for just a few minutes. I might never see that man again.

"Mrs. Rivers-Whitmore?" Fallon's voice cracked through the phone's speaker, startling me.

I pressed the push-to-talk button to answer my assistant. "Yes?"

"Your new client is here."

"Oh. OK. You can send them in," I said, flipping open the folder she'd placed on my desk earlier. I hadn't looked it over yet. I knew nothing about this client. Rushing to scan the details of the case, I read the name on the case files as the client walked in. Stunned and wide-eyed, my head spun from disbelief.

"Zamir." I quickly stood, knocking the file onto the floor. "What are you doing here?"

I crouched to retrieve the folder, giving myself a second to gain at least some of my composure.

When I straightened, our eyes met. He closed the door behind him, slowly stepping toward my desk without taking his eyes off mine.

"Well," he said, moving toward my desk, "I need an attorney." An awkward smile was pressed on his face.

"But, how—"

"I didn't," he cut me off. "I called the firm two weeks ago and was assigned to an attorney named Kerry. I didn't know until I got here that my case had been reassigned to you. I had no idea you worked here until about five minutes ago. Trust me, I am just as surprised as you are."

"Well, I…let me see who else is available to take your case." I reached for the phone.

He reached out as if he was going to touch my hand and then stopped, pulling his hand back. "No. I would like you to take my case." His eyes were pleading.

"Zamir, I don't know if that's a good idea."

"Why not?"

I tilted my head, giving him a knowing look, letting my eyes speak for me.

"What? Because we have history? So?"

I inhaled a long breath, then collapsed into my chair and closed my eyes. "Zamir."

"Blou?"

The sound of my name rolling off his tongue radiated through my body. If just speaking my name shook me to my core, I could only imagine what the effect of his touch might still have on me. A shiver of reminiscence surged through me, coiling at the base of my stomach, sparking light flutters. *Butterflies. Ugh. This was why I couldn't represent him. Blou, focus.*

The only way for me to resist this man had always been to look away and stay stern. "Zamir." Focusing on the vibrant colors in Faith Ringgold's art on the wall behind him, I shook my head. "I can't."

"Blou," he said quietly. "Please. I heard you're the best there is."

My eyes dropped from the painting to him. "So, you did know I worked here." I crossed my arms over my chest, my sharp stare shot daggers of scrutiny.

"No. I overheard someone in the lobby say you're the best, and honestly, it's easy to believe."

My eyebrows lifted. I glared harder. "You expect me to believe that?"

He shrugged. "So, you aren't the best? That would be very odd because from what I remember, you were always exceptional at everything you put your mind to."

I softened, rolling my eyes. A soft smile spread across my face.

"I think things might be awkward between us if we worked together on your…" I glanced down at the closed file. A twinge of self-reproach nudged at my heart. Maybe if I had chosen a firm in DC or New York like he'd suggested, neither of us would be in marital discord right now.

"I'm sorry you're getting a divorce."

"Don't be," he said, taking a seat in front of my desk. "I'm not. And, who feels awkward? I feel fine." He grinned impishly.

"Wait. Why are you in Florida?" I frowned.

"I'll explain all of that once you agree to take my case."

I rolled my eyes, barely managing to stifle the smile that so desperately tugged at the corners of my mouth. "You know I'm married, right?"

His eyes cut to the ring on my finger. "Yep. I noticed it last week and heard it through the gossip vine years ago and, also I... never mind."

"You what?" I asked.

"Don't worry about it. It's not important." Smiling, he slightly tilted his head. "But what *is* important, is your help with my case. What does your marriage have to do with you helping an old friend?" His toothy grin was so contagious that I could no longer contain mine.

I giggled. "You're still a clown." I let out a breathy sigh. "OK. Fine. You've worn me down. I'll take your case."

I stretched my hand toward him, offering a handshake. Beaming,

he took my hand into his. Looking into his dancing eyes, I wondered what stories they held—of years we hadn't shared—the
highs and the lows.

Still holding my hand, he gave it a gentle squeeze.

"Old friend." He smirked.

Chapter *twelve*

"Say what ni?" Neveah's eyebrows lifted, and Aurora gasped.

I was laying across my bed, freshly showered, video chatting with my girls. "Girl, yes. I couldn't believe it. He was the last person I thought would *ever* walk through my door. Especially for me to represent him."

"That's wild," Aurora said, shaking her head as she sipped from a wineglass.

"And you are really going to represent him?" Neveah frowned.

"I mean, yeah. I guess. There's really no reason I couldn't."

She pursed her lips out, twisting them. "No, there's no reason you couldn't," she said, "but there is certainly a reason you shouldn't."

"Neveah, please. It's not going to hurt her to represent her old friend," Aurora piped in. "Plus, this could be fate. If you ask me, they should have never broken up."

"Fate?" Neveah's forehead creased. "Have you forgotten she's still married?"

"To a man who left her, claiming he's sick, and who has a whole love child out there somewhere," she shot back.

"Well, we don't really know that to be true, Ro." Her eyes cut to me, her face softening with empathy.

Aurora kept her eyes on Neveah. "True, but more than likely…"

"OK. Listen. Neveah, it's completely innocent. Zamir was my close friend before we ever dated, and I'm going to help him."

I slid my gaze to Aurora. "Ro, I'm going to get to the bottom of those pictures so I don't have to keep assuming."

"OK, so when do you want us to come over so we can see what else is hidden in that office?"

This time Neveah and Aurora seemed to be on the same page. They both stared into their cameras at me waiting for an answer.

I glanced back and forth between the two of them. "I think I'm going to do this on my own," I said, forcing a smile, "but I know who to call if I fall apart."

For a few seconds, silence filled the space between us.

"Mommy, I want a snack, please."

I smiled at my goddaughter as she appeared in the camera frame. "Hi, princess," I greeted her.

Her radiant smile shifted the somber mood that talking about Gable's secrets left lingering over our girls' chat.

"Hi, godmom! Hi, Tete Veah!"

"Hey, Layla bug!" Neveah waved.
Aurora kissed her pudgy cheek. "OK, y'all. Let me go tend to this little wild one. Blou, call me if you need me. I love y'all."

"We love you too," Neveah and I responded in unison. I blew Layla a kiss, said good night, and ended the call.

I checked my notifications to see who had called and texted me while I had been tied up at work today. I was surprised that Brave hadn't called me asking about the contract. It had slipped my mind to call him earlier to go over what Justin found.

Justin had flagged a few concerns, and I had questions about some of the companies mentioned in the fine print. I scrolled Brave's contact and hit the call icon. His voicemail picked up.

I hung up and sent a quick text:

Me: *Brave, call me as soon as you get this. It's about the contract.*

I rolled out of the bed, pulled on my robe and slipped into my bedroom shoes. As much as I needed to relax, I also couldn't let the night pass without finding out more about what Gable was hiding.

My first session with Dr. Butler today went better than I expected. I felt comfortable with her right away. I chose not to mention that I was planning to go back into the safe today, but I did tell her about the photos I found there.

After confirming what I already knew—I had a lot to unpack—she recommended weekly sessions to start. I agreed. We didn't dig too deeply into my wagon of trauma since it was just the intake session, but after I told her about the panic attacks, she provided me with coping techniques to manage them in the meantime.

As I approached Gable's office door, nerves churned in my stomach. Entering the office, I stopped in the doorway and took a few slow, deep inhales and exhales to settle my nerves and steady the increasing swiftness of my heartbeat.

I decided to start searching the desk drawers this time. I sauntered over and took a seat behind the desk. Running my hand across the surface, I drifted into a flashback of my hands gripping it tightly as Gable leaned my body over, pounding into my wetness with brisk, rhythmic strokes the first day it was delivered. Gable was a strong love maker, but not as bold and zealous as Zamir. The fiery passion Zamir and I shared was beyond the norm of anything I had ever experienced.

I shook my head to banish those intrusive thoughts. *It is insane that you are sitting here comparing the two,* I scolded myself.

I slowly pulled the first drawer open, bracing myself for what I might find. It was empty. I opened drawer after drawer, each one…empty. That was strange. Why would he lock empty drawers? I opened the one that he hadn't locked and slid my hand all the way to the back of the drawer, feeling for something. Anything. Nothing.

With a frustrating breath, I sat back in the chair and closed my eyes, using my body to set the chair in motion, swiveling from side to side. My phone slid off my lap and under the desk.

"Ugh!" Sliding out of the chair and onto my knees, I let out an exasperated sigh. Reaching under the desk for my phone, I twisted my neck to expand my reach. Just as my fingertips grazed it, I caught a glimpse of something shiny. Something silver was flushed against the underside of the open drawer.

I snatched the phone up and straightened. Sliding my fingers beneath the bottom of the drawer, I felt it—a small key taped just out of sight.

I frowned, releasing the key from the tape. Turning it over in my fingers, I studied it, wondering, *What does this…* My words trailed off as my eyes widened.

I turned my body and scooted over to the safe. Sitting in front of it, I contemplated if I really wanted to know what lay beneath the surface of Gable's life with me.

I knew there was something. I just didn't know what. Did I need to know? Would knowing hurt more? I could just walk away now, divorce Gable, and never know what he was hiding—put this all behind us and stay—or if he was really sick and he didn't make it, I could let him take his secrets to the grave.

A tightening twist took hold of my chest; a wave of heat flooded my body. Perspiration seeped into the thin fabric of the gown I wore under my robe. Dr. Butler's voice echoed in my mind as I slipped out of the robe. *Four-seven-eight.* I inhaled for four seconds…held it for seven…exhaled for eight. I repeated it again, then again until the pressure in my chest eased.

As I calmed, I noticed my hand was clenched, slightly trembling, with the key, buried in the palm. I loosened my grip, slowly uncurling my fingers. I sat and stared at the key for what seemed like an eternity before deciding to pull the little box out of the safe and unlock it. I was sure the key belonged to this box.

As I held the box in my hand, I wondered if maybe I shouldn't open it without one of the girls here. I sighed. *You're here now. Might as well get it out of the way.* Listening to my instincts, I stuck the key into the small lock on the box and twisted it. The lock popped open.

Not knowing what Gable was hiding had been driving me insane. Now I had a strong feeling that my curiosity was about to be put to rest, but at what cost? My shattered heart? My broken marriage? Shadowed by an uneasy calm, I felt both relief and anxiety tugging me in opposite directions, relieved that I would finally have some of the answers I'd been searching for and anxious because those answers would force me to face what would come next. Hard truths.

First, peeping into the box, I eased it open. Letters. My heart skipped a beat as I pulled them out. The letters were addressed to Gable at a P.O. Box, with no return address. I thumbed through them searching for the one with the earliest postmark—2018. I pulled the lined paper from its envelope, unfolded it and began to read the neatly written letter:

Gable,

Thank you for agreeing to rent a P.O. Box so that we can keep our conversations as private as possible. And thank you again for giving up so much so that I can have a chance at the life I want with the man that I love.

I swallowed, pushing down the knot forming in my throat.

I know it isn't easy giving up the rights to a child that you created when you've told me how you so deeply desire one of your own. I know your wife is not willing to give that to you, and that makes this even more difficult for you. I appreciate this more than you know.

My fingers tensed around the paper, slightly crinkling the edges. Tears welled in my eyes as I continued to scan every written word.

Even though sending you pictures of him every year around his birthday was the agreement and you insist on updates at least twice a year, I'm still not sure that's a good idea. I think it will make it harder for you. I've seen you shed tears over this—the decision to not only allow me to raise this child with another man but also, being torn over telling her or not.

Barely noticing the gasp that escaped, I covered my mouth with one hand, the letter trembling in the other. The tears that had been lying dormant behind my eyes finally slid down my face.

I know a huge part of your decision was because you don't want to risk losing your wife, but I still think it's best that we have no communication. This is also risky. What if one of our spouses were to find out? We are both doing this to keep our relationships together with the ones we love more than anything else. Please be careful with these letters. With the photos. We both have every-thing to lose. But as long as you insist, I will follow through with my promise.
Thank you for always being such a great friend.
I hope you find the photo enclosed as adorable as I do. He was 7 pounds 6 ounces, 21 inches long.

Your old pal.

I re-read the letter, bewildered, my hands shaking more in-tensely than the time before.

After reading it for a third time, I sat silently staring blankly at the letter, no longer reading. As the shock rolled in then gradually dissipated, an emotionally paralyzing bolt of reality struck me. I couldn't move. I could barely think. For a moment, I couldn't feel.

Cutting through the silence, my cell phone sang out Neveah's ring tone pulling me from the stupor I had sunk into. I wiped my tear-stained face with the back of my hand, let the letter fall to the floor and reached for the phone. I swiped to answer the call.

Suddenly, void of feeling, my voice steady and calm, I spoke into the phone. "It's his."

Chapter **thirteen**

I pulled into Gabriella's driveway, still numb and indifferent but driven by the need for one more answer from her. The flood lights beamed from over the garage, the only lights that cut through the darkness once I killed the headlights.

I snatched the photos and letters from the passenger seat, hopped out of the car and stalked up to the front door. I rang the doorbell twice back-to-back, crossed my arms and waited. The door slowly creaked open. Gabriella appeared wearing a soft green silk robe and an African-print satin bonnet.

"Blou?" She frowned, confusion wrinkling her brow. "What are you doing here?"

"I have a question."

"It's after ten at night," she said, annoyance slipping into her tone. "You could have just called me." Her expression tightened.

The entire drive here, I felt nothing more than hollow. Now, anger—or something close—was beginning to pierce the numbness. As I grew warm, sweat dampened my underarms. Still, I kept my voice low and steady. "I have a question that I need to ask, and I need to do it face to face."

She glared for a beat, then opened the door wider to let me in.

I followed her into the kitchen, lit dimly from the light over the stove.

"Would you like some water?" she asked, walking over to the refrigerator and opening it.

"No, thank you. I'm fine."

She pulled out two bottles anyway, placed one on the counter in front of me, then twisted the cap off the other, taking a small sip.

"What do you want to ask me?" she said, standing across from me. Her jaw clenched.

I shot a piercing look her way. "Did you know?" I tossed the manila envelope across the counter.

Her gaze shifted from the envelope to me. Her brows furrowed. "What is this?" she asked, picking it up and peeking inside.

Arms crossed, my eyes fiercely locked on her, I waited. She slowly emptied the contents of the envelope onto the counter and surveyed the photos. A flicker of confusion illuminated in her eyes.

Her eyes sliding to mine, she cocked her head to the side. "Who is this?"

My jaws flexed. "Gable's baby."

Her eyes grew wide. "What? This can't be…"

"Oh, but it is."

She straightened. "How do you know?"

I picked up the only letter without an envelope—the one I already read—and handed it to her. She held my gaze for a moment, then read. As she raked her eyes across the page, I could see her expression changing with every sentence, her disbelief whittling at every word.

"Wow. Blou." She folded the letter and placed it back with the others that I couldn't bring myself to read yet. "I'm sorry. I didn't know about this."

Looking into her eyes, soft and glossy, I knew she was telling the truth. I released a breath I didn't know I was holding in. The tension I carried into her kitchen just moments earlier surrendered to a quiet melancholy.

I gathered the photos and letters and slid them back into the envelope. "Thank you. That's all I needed to know," I murmured, turning to leave. "I'll let you get back to your evening."

"Blou, wait." Gabriella soothingly placed her hand on my shoulder. I turned back. Tactically avoiding her eyes, I set my sights on the center piece of roses carefully arranged in the vase on the counter.

"Are you OK?" she asked softly.

I smiled ruefully. "No. But I've suffered a lot of loss, Gabriella. I'm sure I'll be fine."

With a sharp turn, I moved toward the front door then turned to face Gabriella. She was right behind me. "I'm sorry. I shouldn't have come over here unannounced. Good night." I hurried out the door and to my car.

It had started to rain. I flung my car door open, quickly jumped in, and sank into my seat, closing my eyes. So many emotions surged through my body, I didn't know which I felt the heaviest. Tears stung my eyes. I didn't know what to do next. I felt like screaming, crying, and breaking something all at once, but I also wanted to hold it all in—swallow every feeling, all the pain, the aching that had been naggingly present since this all began.

I pulled out of the driveway, turning my wipers on. The rain poured harder from the darkest skies, matching the somber heaviness that filled every inch of my body, mind, and soul, crushing my once beatific spirit. I wiped tears, focusing my eyes to see through the rain the best I could. There were no streetlights illuminating the blackness, only my car's headlights shining.

I reached into the middle console, quickly glancing down for a tissue. Looking back at the road, a deer was crossing ahead of me.

"Oh, God!" I slammed on the brakes, barely missing it. I slowly pulled off to the side of the road, simultaneously consumed with both fear and relief. Trembling, I laid my head on the steering wheel. The rain pounded the windshield, echoing my pounding heart. Taking slow breaths to calm the rhythm, I said a silent, *Thank You, God.*

I jumped at the sharp sound of my phone ringing. Aunt Gina's number flashed across my dash. At this point, I no longer wanted to hide the truth from her. I needed her sound guidance. If anybody could help me sort through all this chaos, it was her, so I answered. "Hello." My voice cracked.

"Blou." Aunt Gina's cracking voice matched mine.

"It's Brave. He's in the hospital."

Soaked from the hammering rain, I hurried through the emergency room doors of Parksdale South hospital. I hated hospitals. Spent a lot of time here when my father was sick.

Four years before then, I'd sat coloring in the waiting area with Aunt Gina on the maternity ward when my mom was in labor with Brave. The wounding memory of that day came back to me so clearly, as if it was just yesterday. That day started as one of the best days of our lives. But it ended as one of the worst days of mine.

I could never forget the agony on my father's face when he stepped inside the waiting room—the one reserved just for those waiting for the debut of their newest member of their family. Aunt Gina and I jumped up, first excited that he had come with the news we had been waiting for.

But we had quickly realized from the pain in his expression that he didn't come to bear the news we were expecting.

My father had moved toward me and pulled me into his arms. He stared down at the floor, his mouth parted, but no words came. Fear seeped into my stomach and climbed steadily into my chest.

"Dad…what's wrong?" I'd asked softly.

"Elias, is the baby OK?" Aunt Gina had asked, stepping beside us.

My dad nodded slowly. "It's Ci…Ci." Tears had welled in his eyes and rolled down his cheeks.

"Elias, what is wrong with Cicely?"
Aunt Gina asked, her voice laced with panic.

"Blou," a familiar voice called from behind me.

Jolted back into the present, I turned towards the direction of the baritone voice calling me. Uncle Lance approached, taking me into a warm embrace.

"Hey, Blou Bear. How are you?"

I stayed wrapped in his arms for a moment longer than I expected.

Realizing that tears were hanging in the corners of my eyes, I quickly wiped them before pulling back. I gazed up at my uncle, his hair peppered with more grays since the last time I saw him a month ago. His tired eyes exposed the worry he carried.

"I'm fine, Unc. I got here as fast as I could in this storm," I said, omitting the deer incident. "How is Brave? What happened?"

"He's OK. Banged up pretty bad. They just finished x-rays and are getting him patched up. Gina's back there with him now."

Relief washed over me. "What happened?" I asked again.

"I'm not completely sure of all the details. Something about Tyrek, some other guy, and a contract. Some crypto-something or 'nother."

I frowned. "What?"

"Yeah. I guess your brother is doing some business with them, Brave got angry about something, and it turned ugly."

My nostrils flared. "I know he didn't," I muttered under my breath.

"What was that, suga?"

I shook my head. "Um. Nothing, Unc. Are they letting any more visitors back?"

"Yes. Three at a time. I was just waiting here for you to arrive. Come on."

He moved toward the double doors and nodded at the young lady behind the curved desk as she pressed a button to let us through.

"You're already a familiar face around here I see," I teased.

He chuckled. "Yeah, I guess so. I've been back and forth through these doors for one reason or another. First, your aunt needed her sweater out the car, then she needed a snack—after a while I figured I'd come on out here and wait for you."

The door to Brave's room was slightly ajar. Uncle Lance gave it a light knock before sticking his head in and then pushing it open. I stepped into the room, willing myself to soften my face. I was fuming inside thinking about what Uncle Lance told me, hoping for Brave's sake, he hadn't done what I suspected. If he had messed up my money, I swear, I would be done with him. He had never called me back after I called and texted him about Justin's concerns about the contract. *What did he do? Had he involved Tyrek after he promised he wouldn't? I was going to kill him.*

I nearly gasped when I saw Brave lying there, face bruised and swollen. Every shred of anger I felt instantly left me.

"Brave, oh my God." I rushed to his bedside.

"I'm so sorry, Blou," he said, voice cracking, gaze fixed straight ahead, unshed tears threatening to fall.

Most days, just the thought of him stirred resentment in me, but for the first time in a long while, I felt something other than anger toward him. The only time I ever remembered feeling happy at the thought of Brave was when my mom was pregnant with him. For seven short months, I loved him more than anything.

I was so excited to welcome my baby brother into the world, especially proud that I was included in naming him. We came up with his name one afternoon while out for ice cream. My mom's cravings were very unorthodox. She wanted pickles with everything, keeping a snack bag of them tucked in her purse.

At the ice cream shop, she was eating chocolate ice cream and pickles.

"Ew. Yuck. That baby is so brave." My nose wrinkled with disgust. "If I was in your tummy, I would not be eating that."

We all laughed. She had playfully smeared a dot of chocolate ice cream on my nose. Wiping the ice cream from my face with a napkin, my dad said, "Well, I guess we have us a brave little boy then, huh?"

My mom giggled, biting into her pickle. As she swallowed, her face lit up with recognition, a sparkle in her eye. My dad and I had caught the look immediately as if we had read her mind. In perfect unison, the three of us said, "Brave."

A wide smile spread on my mom's face; her dimples popped with contentment. "Yes," she said. "Let's name him, Brave."

I grinned, toothy and overjoyed. "Brave Rivers." I said proudly.

The doctor stepped into the room interrupting my thoughts. She smiled faintly as her eyes locked with mine. She turned her attention to Brave. "Mr. Rivers, do you need anyone to step out of the room as I update you on your condition?

He winced in pain as he shook his head. "No. Everyone here is good."

"OK," she begins. "You have a slight concussion and a fractured rib." Her eyes were soft. "We need to keep you overnight for observation."

Brave nodded but remained quiet.

"The nurse will be back in soon to administer more pain medicine to keep you comfortable."

I kept my eyes on Brave as she moved toward the door to leave. Both confusion and sadness clutching my aching heart. My chest stung from the harsh familiarity of this hospital where my mom died. The same hospital where I sat by my dad's side day after day, the beeping machines taunting me with the reminder that his days were short. Now, here I was again, back here, feeling sorry for the one person who was the reason why I was going through every hard thing in my life alone without my mother.

Anger settled quietly back into its usual space in my heart. My jaws hardened. *More than likely, the reason he was in this mess was because of something he did wrong.* I thought.

"What did you do?" I asked through teeth clenched. Flooded with a paradox of emotions, I glared at him, my breathing becoming short and winded.

"I..." Brave started.

I held up my hand. "You know what? Just save it. I don't even want to hear your voice right now."

"Blou," Aunt Gina said softly, moving beside me. She placed a comforting hand on my back, but I no longer wanted to be comforted. I needed refuge—to escape this place, it's brutal memories. To escape Brave and whatever it was that he did to screw up my life this time. To escape the conflicting urge to either empathize with him or cling tighter to my indignation. To relieve the grip of guilt that firmly hugged my dry throat each time my dad would look at me with those pleading eyes that begged me to show my brother some compassion.

 I couldn't stay.

"I'm done." I turned and moved swiftly toward the door.

"Blou," Aunt Gina's voice called after me.

I didn't mean any disrespect to my aunt, but I couldn't turn back. I moved briskly down the hall, and through the double doors. The unrelenting juxtaposition of emotions followed like a shadow.

On the other side of the door, I bolted toward the exit with my head down, forcing back tears, praying that my racing heart and the constriction forming in my chest would not spiral into a full-blown panic attack.

"These sensations you are feeling are temporary and they will pass." I echoed Dr. Butler's words under my breath.

Just as I reached the exit doors, I bumped into a firm body. Strong arms gently wrapped around my waist to catch my fall. A familiar smell of fruity, yet woody and musky scents filled my nose.

"I—I'm so sorr—" I glanced up and our eyes collided.
For a moment, I was locked into his gaze, lips parted, speechless. The busyness of the hospital dulled into a distant buzz. Steadying myself, I broke free from the grip that held me up and stepped back. His eyes held mine in place.

"Zamir," I whispered softly. "Wh-What are you doing here?" I tilted my head slightly. For a second, I thought maybe…maybe he was here for me. I shook that thought away. That would be ridiculous. Even if he wanted to be here for me, how would he have even known I was here?

"Blou, it's nice to see you." Though his smile barely reached his eyes, the spark radiating between us said he meant it. "My son is here being seen."

"Oh." I glanced around. I didn't know what his soon-to-be ex-wife looked like, but there wasn't anyone standing close by who seemed to be with him. "Is he OK?"

"*Um*. Yes. He will be."

In our initial meeting, he did mention that he had a son. He didn't talk much about him, other than he wanted to make sure he got joint custody with a fifty/fifty split. He didn't think there would be much of a fight, but he and his estranged wife had not spoken much since the separation. He believed the entire divorce process would go amicably.

Silence lingered between us. I shifted my weight from one foot to the other. Then, as if a light was switched on in his head, concern creased his brows. "Why are you here?"

I looked away. I didn't want to get into my family drama, not now and definitely not here. "My brother is here. He's OK though—just a little accident."

He smirked, a nostalgic beam in his eyes. "Little bro Brave. I haven't seen him in forever. When we came home for spring break—2017, to be exact."

I forced a smile. "Yeah, it's been a while," I said.

Desperate to escape this hospital and this awkward but magnetic current between us, I rushed to end the small talk. "It was good seeing you. I have to get going, but I'll see you in two weeks for our meeting to prepare for your mediation."

"Sure thing. I gotta get back in here anyway." His mouth slowly turned up into a warm smile. "See you later, Blou Skies."

A flutter tickled my stomach. *You are my Blou skies when my life is cloudy.* The first time he'd whispered those words to me was the summer after our high school graduation. We'd sat on the beach watching the sunset, our place of retreat after an argument between him and his dad who wanted him to stay close to home for college—didn't think it was a good idea for him to go so far away at such a young age. Zamir was adamant about attending Howard. We had become close friends, since we'd met outside the movie theater the summer before. He was my person. I was his. He wanted more. I didn't want to risk our friendship. After the first time I heard those words, it became his favorite thing to say to me and my favorite thing to hear.

A tender smile spread across my face. "Good night, Zamir," I said, before turning and walking away, feeling his eyes following me.

Chapter *fourteen*

To Blou, My One True Love,

Let me start by saying I'm sorry. I never meant for you to find out like this. Gabriella called and told me you stopped by. She was extremely upset with me as well. Of course, she has forgiven me, and I hope you can too. It's a long story. Too much to put into a letter but I do want you to know that after the night I asked you to marry me, I have never been with another woman.

I couldn't tell you about the baby and risk losing you. She felt the same about the man she married, so we made a decision that was best for all of us. She and I were good friends and have been since college, but we just weren't compatible for anything more solid or a long-term commitment for several reasons. But you and I...we work, in almost every aspect.
Please forgive me.

Also, my condition is not responding to the medication as they—we—hoped it would. I have been declining rapidly. They increased the dosage, and maybe—hopefully—we will see a change for the better within the next couple of weeks. Right now, not so much. If I make it out of here alive and well, I will make all of this up to you if you let me.

Please forgive me.
Love, Gable

I balled up the letter and threw it across the bedroom, then grabbed a pillow, buried my face into it, and released a deep, guttural scream.

This letter did nothing to help me. It didn't make me want to forgive him. This man was unbelievable: *I know I left you but forgive me. I know I've had a secret child for our entire marriage, but forgive me.* Yada, yada, yada. And what did he mean, *almost,* every aspect? Was he referring to my unwillingness to have a child?

My mom and dad leaving me was out of their control. Even my break up with Zamir was mutual, for the most part, even though I'd always felt he could have fought harder. He could have come home with me instead of staying up North if I meant as much to him as he'd said. We kind of left each other. But this, this was just not right. Concealing a child from me—from his sister—that was crucial. Inconsiderate. Deceitful.

Neveah's ring tone chimed.

"Hello," I answered tersely.

"Whoa," she said. "What's up with you?"

"Gable can go straight to hell," I snapped and immediately regretted it.

Neveah gasped. "Girl, I don't know if that's an appropriate thing to say given his—"

Closing my eyes tight, I threw myself back onto the bed. "I know, I know." I moaned. "I shouldn't have said that."

"You want to talk about it?" Neveah asked.

"He just makes me so mad in these letters, and this last one was even more infuriating. He keeps asking for my forgiveness like he didn't just rip my heart out and stomp all over it twice within a month's time."

An alarm sounded, reminding me of my therapy appointment. It had been a couple weeks since Brave's incident and my last unexpected run in with Zamir. I had plenty to talk about.

"Oh. Listen, I gotta go. I have to log on for my virtual therapy session."

"Therapy?" Neveah said, her tone shooting up. "Girl, when did you start therapy?"

"Bye. I'll call you back." I rushed off the phone.

I logged into the portal and clicked the link to begin my session. Dr. Butler was already there.

"Hi there, Blou," she greeted me with a smile.

"Hi, Dr. Butler. I'm sorry about the cancellation last week. I had a last-minute deposition that got thrown on my calendar."

She smiled. "No worries. I understand the life of an attorney." How are you feeling today?" she asked.

"Honestly? All over the place." Tears welled up behind my eyes. "I can't even pin down just one emotion that I'm feeling."

She nodded. "That's OK. It's completely normal to feel several different emotions simultaneously and for some of those emotions to be opposing. Let's talk about what has you feeling all over the place."

Her eyes held a steady warmth, anchoring me in place and offering a sense of safety I needed to pour out my most vulnerable thoughts. I unraveled thread by thread all I'd been holding inside. I gave her the rundown about my encounters with Zamir, Brave's irresponsible behavior, Gable's baby, his illness and the letters.

Cutting in with care, Dr. Butler asked questions that delved further into my unresolved feelings for Zamir, cast a mirror to the resentment I harbored toward Brave, and probed into the ache of the most pressing matter—Gable, his load of baggage, and half-hearted apologies.

By the end of the session, I had become highly aware of a few things: My feelings for Zamir didn't just return the night I saw him but had lingered dormant in places I hadn't touched. My resentment toward Brave had more to do with my own unresolved perspective than it had to do with Brave, and I had a lot more processing to do concerning the mess of my marriage.

Holding on to resentment, crumpling letters, and sweeping feelings under the rug would not move my healing forward. I had work to do. Although, I wasn't quite sure if I was ready to discuss my biggest skeleton yet. The reason I've carried guilt and shame for so long.

After disconnecting my call with Dr. Butler, I decided to look over Zamir's file, which I bought home from the office, to give it a final look before mediation tomorrow.

Fallon had sent over a corrigendum to the other party's attorney to have her correct a mistake in the custody agreement, but an updated copy was not in the file. I checked my email to see if Fallon had sent it to me.

There was an email from Zamir. I clicked it open. He asked if we could meet tonight to discuss some things ahead of the mediation tomorrow. *He wanted to meet outside of the office?* My stomach did a sharp back flip. *Girl, you have to keep this professional. He's your client.* I thought about his request briefly, drumming my fingers on the desk, pondering my response.

The doorbell rang. I frowned. I wasn't sure who it could be. I checked the camera as I always did when someone was at my door.

It was Aurora and Neveah. I slapped my forehead. It had totally slipped my mind that we had planned to eat dinner together here tonight.

I typed a quick text message to Zamir instead of replying to his email.

Me: *I'm sorry, I can't tonight. Are you available to meet in the morning for coffee prior to the mediation?*

The doorbell rang again. I closed the laptop and headed to the door.

"Girl, it took you long enough," Aurora snapped, pushing past me with a bag of food in her hands.

I rolled my eyes. "So rude."

Neveah giggled as she hugged me before moving toward the kitchen with a denim Telfar duffle on her shoulder. I followed.

"Honestly, I forgot y'all were coming over. I didn't add it to my calendar when we planned it last week."

"It's OK, sis. We know you have a lot going on," Neveah said, side-eyeing Aurora. "If I had known you forgot, I would've mentioned when we spoke earlier."

"I was just messing with you." She moved toward me, arms outstretched. "Give me a hug, pookie." She wrapped her arms around me. A light fruity fragrance with a hint of coconut, vanilla and something else I couldn't quite put my finger on whiffed the air.

"Girl, gone now." We laughed as I gently pushed her away. "All jokes aside though. What perfume are you wearing?"

"I'm just wearing body glaze. Brown Honey. It's from this company I saw on social media called Canvas Beauty. I had to see what the hype was about."

"Well, it didn't disappoint, babe."

"Why, thank you, my darling." She batted her eyes.

"Umm-hmm," Neveah hummed. "I told her to send me the link. Y'all know I love me a good body glaze too."

"Enough about the body glaze. Girl, let me get that BLKX-CLLNC crop top you're wearing. It's giving I'm black and I'm proud, with a whole lot of confidence." Aurora said, gently tugging at the bottom of my crop.

"*Um-hm.*" Neveah co-signed Aurora's compliment. "That Carolina blue is a nice color. I have the black one."

"Thank you both." I said, smiling at the amount of hyping each other up my friends and I do. "Y'all rode here together?" I asked.

"No. We just got here at the same time. I'm going to stay the night, if that's okay with you," Neveah said.

"Now, when have you ever asked me can you stay over?" I teased. "But of course."

"Is Lukas on a business trip or something?" Aurora asked.

"No. He took his children on vacation for spring break," she said, spooning rice and peas, cabbage, and oxtail on three paper plates. She wasted no time unpacking the food. "Y'all want plantains?"

Aurora and I looked at each other then back at Neveah.

"Why didn't you go?" I asked, ignoring her question.

She shrugged. "I'm not ready to go on a weeklong vacation with his kids. Do you want plantains?"

"Yes," we said in unison.

Aurora's brows furrowed. "But you've been around them several times."

"Yeah, but a weeklong vacation is different. I mean, he felt some kind of way because I declined the invite, but I don't think I'm ready for that." She grabbed a fork, took a plate, and sat at the table.

"Where did he take them?" I asked, picking up a plate and sitting next to her.

"Jamaica."

Aurora smirked. "So that's why you asked me to pick up Jamaican food, because you missed your bae, and deep down, you wish you would have gone on that trip, but you're afraid of commitment, so you're pushing that good man and his kids away?" she said, rushing her words out.

"Dang, girl." I laughed. "Slow down and breathe."

"Let's just bless the food, Ms. Analytical." Neveah reached for our hands and nodded at Aurora to pray.

"Dear God, thank You for this sisterhood. I pray our love for You and one another only grows stronger. During our trials, help us lean on You instead of our own understanding. And we ask that you bless the food that we are about to receive. We are forever grateful. We love You, God. In Your son, Jesus' name we pray. Amen."

"Amen," Neveah and I echoed.

"So, you go to therapy now, huh?" Neveah glanced at me and then back at her plate, poking at the cabbage with her fork.

I stuffed a forkful of savory oxtail into my mouth and slowly chewed, not really wanting to get into too much detail about my therapy session.

Swallowing, my gaze drifted to her. "Um. Yeah. I started a few weeks ago."

"I think that's awesome," Aurora said.

Neveah nodded in agreement. "Yeah."

"But let me tell y'all about this last letter I got from Gable." I put my fork down and sat back in my chair."

"Oh, yeah. You never got around to telling me the details." Neveah wiped her mouth and pushed her plate to the side, giving me her full attention.

"Are y'all sitting down?" I asked, a smirk playing on my lips.

They both chuckled. "Girl, clearly, we are. What it say?" Aurora asked, leaning in, her eyes trained on me, waiting for me to spill the steadily brewing tea of my life.

"Let me just read it to you." I raced to my bedroom, grabbed the ball of paper from the floor and headed back to the table.

They eyed the crumpled paper but held their thoughts.

I read the letter word for word. Their expressions changed with each twist and turn of the implausible audacity etched onto the paper. For the first time, I noticed how the handwriting was just as chaotic as the thoughts that were poured onto this letter. Each word's strokes were inconsistent as if written with a shaky hand. Much different from the other letters—those two were more accurate reflections of Gable's flawless handwriting. A nudge of empathy melted the ice in a small corner of my heart.

Neveah pursed her lips. "Now, you know I'm usually Team Gable, but he tried it."

"Right," Aurora agreed, "but B, if we're being honest, Gable has always been controlling and a little inconsiderate of your feelings—in a nice-nasty way. The whole, I-did-what's-best-for-us tactics are nothing new."

My expression tightened. "What do you mean?" I asked. Aurora was not the one for walking on eggshells. I knew whether I liked what she was going to say or not, she was going to say it.

Her expression soft, she slightly tilted her head and bit her bottom lip. "I mean this in the most caring way: He's always been selfish. He decided when y'all were officially a couple, which came with a proposal the same day. You weren't ready to marry him so soon, but he pushed it anyway. You wanted a totally different house; he said this one was better for y'all. You wanted to go for partner at the firm. What did he say? A partner position was for a man or a single woman who never planned to marry or have a family, so you sacrificed a dream—no compromise. I could go on and on. You've gone along with any and everything he's wanted."

"Well," Neveah cut in, "not really. He wanted a child and—"

"Correct," Aurora said, pointing at Neveah, "and she refused to give him that, so out of guilt she just went along with whatever *else* he wanted, and I think he knows that, and he plays on it."

I open my mouth to object. "Mmm. I—"

"And," Aurora continued, holding up a finger, "that's why he slid in that part about y'all work in *almost* every aspect. He wanted to remind you that you didn't give him the thing he wanted the most. And married or not, he cheated, which he makes no attempt at accountability for in that letter."

I looked at Neveah for her rebuttal to what Aurora was saying. Catching my glance, she looked down at her plate.

"You agree with her?" I asked in disbelief.

She shrugged. "Well, she's kinda on point with most of what she said, sis," she said gently.

"If she was with the man who she really wanted, I guarantee you she would have gone to therapy, worked through her trauma, and popped that man out a baby—or two, or three," Aurora said smugly.

"Hello." I waved. "She is still in the room."

Neveah shot her a pointed look. "Now Ro, you just had to go too far."

I sat quietly for a moment, then suddenly giggles erupted from deep in my belly, a ripple at first, then a burst of laughter. Tears streamed down my face as I tumbled over onto the floor consumed by uncontrollable hysterics. The joviality of the moment must have been infectious because the girls joined my laughing fit. The cachinnation had us all in tears.

Once the giggles subsided, a comfortable silence fell over us. I released a loud sigh.

Shifting my gaze to Aurora, I offered her a faint smile. "All jokes aside, you might be right, Ro," I said. "Maybe I've been living in this fantasy land I've made up in my head. Maybe I've been avoiding the truth to keep my idea of the perfect marriage I wanted us to have intact." I paused, slowly exhaling a soft sigh. "I never wanted to admit it, but something has always seemed to be missing. But for the most part, I've been happy with Gable. What you said though, it makes sense. That's a perspective I will gladly talk over with my therapist."

My relationship with Zamir ended because I chose me. I could have easily stayed North to be with him. Even though he didn't press me to stay, I knew he wanted me to. And maybe if he had pushed more, I would have stayed. Maybe if he said the right things… When I walked away, I was torn between if I was making the right decision or not. When I met Gable, he took the lead and pressed me to make decisions that aligned with what he wanted—some of what I wanted too. I thought Zamir didn't try hard enough to keep me with him, so it was easier to resist doing what he wanted me to do, while Gable was more persistent. Until now, I'd never questioned it. Maybe loving someone means allowing them to find their way and follow their dreams and in time they would come back to you if it was meant to be.

But wasn't that kind of what Gable was doing now? He said in a letter that if it was too hard for me to wait for his outcome, then he understood if I moved on. I just wasn't sure if I could really believe he meant that. It's the total opposite of who Gable had shown me he was. I'd never known him to give up something he really wanted. Maybe he didn't want me anymore. He asked for my forgiveness, said he would rather me wait but gave me his blessing to move on. I didn't know what was real between Gable and me anymore. Somberness weighed heavier on my already weary mind.

My phone dinged with a text notification. It was Zamir. A swift thud quickened my heart at the sight of his name on my screen.

Zamir: *Sure thing. I'm always down for some coffee and a little reflection. Good night, and see you soon, Blou Skies. *Wink emoji.**

I blushed, rolling my eyes at the text. When I glanced up, both Aurora and Neveah were eyeballing me. The flattery quickly faded. Suddenly, I felt exposed under their piercing stares. I pushed myself from the floor and straightened. Their eyes followed me. I knew from the looks on their faces that they were not about to drop this.

"What?" I murmured, fidgeting with the long sleeve of my lounge shirt.

Neveah stood, Aurora followed. "Who was that?" Aurora questioned.

"A client," I answered, eyes averted, avoiding theirs.

Neveah placed a hand on her hip, shaking her head slowly. "Girl, don't play with us. That was Zamir, wasn't it?"

"I mean, he is my client." I busied myself clearing the table. Their eyes moved with me as I went from the table to the kitchen sink, grabbed a dish cloth, dampened it, and glided back to the table.

Deep down, I knew taking Zamir on as a client meant keeping a physical distance from him intimately, but he drew me in emotionally every time I saw him. There was a mutual craving lingering between us since high school, one that I thought had resolved through time and distance.

Groaning, I dramatically sank into a chair, resting my head on the table. "That man still drives me crazy, y'all—in a good way. But in a way I don't want to feel because given my circumstances, it's also bad to feel this way."

"He's your client," Neveah reminded me as if I could forget that.

I tightened my lips, sulking in my rising frustration. I hated that she kept reminding me of that. She was always the voice of reason, but sometimes that reasoning was bothersome. Mixing logic with emotions didn't always make sense, and trying to make it make sense just overcomplicated things. Even if I wasn't representing Zamir, I was still married, so the constant recall of our professional status was a tad bit annoying.

I gave her a knowing look. "I know, I know, and I'm not going to cross any lines, Veah." Catching the grating shift in my tone, I softened quickly, releasing the annoyance I felt. Neveah genuinely meant well, and she was doing what she did best—help and protect.

Letting my shoulders sag, I blinked rapidly, fighting back tears. "But that's really the least of my worries. I have no idea what I'm going to do about Gable, y'all. I go back and forth about what I would do if he came home. Maybe I could have forgiven him for leaving the way he did, but I don't think I have enough grace in me to get past the secret baby."

Aurora placed a soothing hand on my back. "You definitely have a lot to figure out, my friend."

"I do." I said, straightening, "and that's why Zamir should be the least of y'all worries."

Aurora frowned. "Girl, I ain't worried about Zamir." She pointed at Neveah. "That's all her."

Neveah shot her a heated glare.

"Besides," Aurora continued, "why is he getting divorced?"

Slicing her with a side eye, I cocked my head. "Mm. Now you know I can't tell you that. It's called confidentiality."

She shrugged. "I know. It didn't hurt to try though."

I shook my head. "I wouldn't expect anything less," I said, nudging her playfully.

Not that I could give out any details of his case, but Zamir hadn't even told me what caused the divorce, and I hadn't pushed him. I was representing him so I figured if he wanted to share the details he would. The divorce didn't seem like it would get ugly. They seemed to have agreed on most things, so I didn't need to know. He just wanted a lawyer present to make sure everything was fair for him.

I picked up my phone and scrolled to the last text he had sent me.

I typed, *Good night. See you in the morning. *Blush emoji.*
Deleted the blush emoji. *Smile emoji.*
Send.

Chapter *fifteen*

I picked a booth by the window at the café where Zamir, and I had agreed to meet. The dainty shop was close to the firm so we could walk over for mediation. Zamir had texted me that he would be running about five minutes late. I don't like wasting time on a workday, but I was grateful that he at least let me know instead of having me waiting with no heads-up. His tardiness also gave me a chance to respond to some texts and emails.

I rolled my eyes when Brave's name flashed across my screen. I sent the call to voicemail. He had been blowing my phone up since he'd gotten out of the hospital. Last night, I'd learned from Aunt Gina that he was staying at her house until his broken leg healed. I didn't notice anything wrong with his leg when I was at the hospital. I thought he only had a concussion and fractured rib. I also could barely see past my anger at the time.

She gently encouraged me to talk to him. She reminded me of my dad in the way that she nudged me toward Brave in the most loving ways. But without even hearing the full story, I knew Brave had broken his promise to me in one way or another. I didn't have the mental capacity to deal with him right now.

"Hey, hey, hey."

My heart leaped at the sound of the deep, familiar voice. Sliding my gaze from my phone to his beautiful chocolate face, I dropped my phone into the brown leather Tian Zevon mini tote I'd recently purchased online during some much needed retail therapy. I couldn't help but notice how the white collared button down Zamir wore complemented his broad shoulders and well-defined chest, giving away the strength of his frame. He towered over me as if he was waiting for something.

"Oh." I blushed and stood to hug him. As he wrapped his strong arms around me, warmth spread through me. His body was still just the right balance of hardness and softness, which I had secretly appreciated back in high school when he would grab me in a playful embrace. But my nerves especially tingled from the reminder of what he felt like in college when he'd hold me closer, more intimately, drawing me inside of his affectionate soul.

He planted a soft kiss on my forehead before releasing me, evoking waves of electricity down my spine. A brief tremble shook my body.

"Um. OK. Let's get st-started." Fumbling over my words, I took my seat. Zamir slid into the booth across from me, amusement dancing in his eyes. *Oh God. Did he notice how my body shook?* My cheeks warmed with embarrassment.

I cleared my throat. "So what did you want to talk about?" I asked.

He picked up the cup of coffee in front of him and sipped it. His eyes locked on mine, he smirked.

"I went ahead and ordered for you. I hope you don't mind."

"I'm impressed." He grinned widely. "You remember exactly how I like my coffee." His eyes flickered with something I wasn't sure of.

Breaking free from the unreadable messages in his eyes, I averted my gaze to my chai tea latte. Picking it up, I asked, "So what's up?"

He sighed heavily. "We've discussed the divorce on a professional level," he began, "but I wanted to talk to you as a friend."

I nodded, taking a slow sip of my warm drink. "When I got married to Esa, I loved her. I didn't marry her to get divorced. I meant for my vows to be forever."

I leaned forward, lifting my hands gently. "Zamir, you don't need to—"

He shook his head. "It's OK. Please. Let me finish."

I relaxed in my seat.

For a second, he hesitated, drawing in a short breath, then exhaling. "But," he paused, shaking his head. His eyes laced with pain as he spoke his next words. "What she did. I can't...Love isn't enough to stay."

My eyes stung. A familiar pain radiating from his eyes mirrored the same ache in mine, which reflected back each time I've gazed in the mirror since Gable left.

His lips parted, but the words were lost in his throat. I sat quietly, patiently waiting until he found them.

"Blou, I know this might not be appropriate to say, but I'm going to say it anyway because so much went unsaid between us when we broke up." His eyes found mine. I locked into his gaze as he spoke. "I had to fight so hard to love someone else other than you. When I got transferred to the Florida office, I—"

"Wait, what?" I interrupted. "When?"

"About a month after you left DC."

My eyes narrowed, jaws tensed. I carefully choose my words to emerge softer than the thud in my heart.

"You moved here right after me and you didn't think to let me know?" My tone was sharp but hushed.

His brow raised. "You wouldn't answer my calls, and you never replied to texts, remember? I left several messages. Now I know you never listened to them."

His wounded gaze softened my stance. I swallowed the heated response that sat on the tip of my tongue. There was nothing I could say to that. He was right. Those messages still sat unheard, in my cloud storage. I muted text messages from him, and whenever I scrolled past them, I deleted the thread without opening them. Eventually, they stopped coming.

He continued. "The day after I got here, I went by Aunt Gina's and—"

I tilted my head, baffled. "Aunt Gina never told me you came by." I crossed my arms over my chest.

"I didn't talk to her. A guy was in the driveway when I got there. There were quite a few cars there, so she must have been having a party of some kind." He leaned forward. "He asked if he could help me with anything. I introduced myself, told him I was there to see you. He offered a handshake and said he'd heard a lot about me. Introduced himself as your husband. Said you had gone to the store and might be awhile, but he would tell you I came by."

My brows furrowed in confusion. Then, suddenly it hit me. It must have been Neveah's surprise birthday cookout at Aunt Gina's. We'd planned for her a couple of months after I moved back. That was early February. But Gable and I weren't even official, according to him. I remembered everything about that day. We'd forgotten to pick up the cake on the way over to Aunt Gina's. I had sent Gable to get it. He must have been returning when Zamir came by because Gable had been gone for so long everyone had arrived before he returned. He had lied. I definitely wasn't gone to the store.

Zamir kept going. "I didn't want to disrupt your life. You were married—or it looked that way. I left and decided it was best to move on with my life the best I could without you. A couple of days later I met Esa. She was…she was nice and fun. We clicked from the moment we met, and I liked having her around, so…I mean…it wasn't the same as when I met you, but it was something. It felt good—eased the pain of losing you."

I shifted in my seat, a swift somersault curling in my gut. Nausea stirred. Interlocking my fingers to keep my hands from trembling from a new reality, I placed them firmly on the table.
Zamir's gaze shifted toward my hands. Frowning, he reached over and gently pulled them apart.

"You aren't wearing your ring?"

His questioning eyes lingered on my bare ring finger, then traveled to meet my misty eyes. This was too much.

When I met Gable, I didn't hold anything back. I gave him everything—my history with Zamir, my entire truth. I couldn't believe it took Zamir to show up for him to want something official. No wonder he was hard pressed about getting married so quickly. He felt threatened and never told me why. All these years had gone by, and I never knew he'd met Zamir.

My heart picked up its beat; the chatter around us faded to the background. My mind willed me to breathe, my lungs begging for air, but my body rebelled.

Oh no. Don't do this Blou. Just breathe.

I hadn't noticed Zamir move. Now he sat beside me, arm draped around my shoulders. Sliding his fingers between mine, he pulled me in close, just like he'd done since our senior year in high school whenever panic took me by surprise. My labored breathing had always calmed under subjection to his touch. He still had that effect on me. I rested my head against his firm chest, taking in the warm, smoky, citrus scent of his cologne with each slow inhale. His chest slowly rose and fell with a melody that lulled my heartbeat back to its steady beat.

"Well, hey there, Blou." I looked up to see Gabriella, her jaw clenched, her narrowed eyes burning into me.

"Um. Hey," I said, straightening, pulling back from Zamir's embrace. Our locked fingers fell apart.

She looked from me to Zamir, then back to me.

"So…this is what you're doing while my brother is fighting for his life?" she snarled. "Hugged up with some other man."

I glanced around, hoping that no one could hear her accusations. "Gabriella, it's not what you think," I said in a hushed tone, careful not to draw attention.

Stepping closer, she placed a hand on her hip. "Well, just what is it then because what I think is just what it looks like."

After the panic attack, seeing Gabriella here spun me a little more than I was already.

Regaining my composure, my defenses woke up. A rush of heat surged through me. Before I could stop the anger that had taken residence inside me for weeks, I regurgitated heated words in her direction.

"Excuse, me?" If Zamir wasn't in the way I would have stood To meet her gaze at eye level. Still, I peered at her with fiery eyes, with just as much intensity as hers carried.

"With everything your brother has put me through—correction, *is* putting me through, you have the audacity to stand here and judge me based off an assumption? I don't owe you any explanations." I smirked. "Just like you don't owe me any."

She winched as if the truth behind my words stung.

Zamir's hand gently rested on my lower back—the instinctive way he reminded me to keep my cool after witnessing me losing my temper a few times, but I didn't want to calm down. She had some nerve.

Her jaws softened, her eyes withdrew sightly. "He might be dying, Blou." A slight edge still lingered in her tone. "The treatment isn't working. His condition seems to be worsening. I was able to go see him, and he doesn't look—"

"Tuh. I thought there was no visitation, per the contract." I smirked, using quotation fingers.

"I—"

I raised a hand. I wasn't interested in hearing the excuse, reason, or whatever she was about to give. "Gabriella, honestly, that's neither here nor there at this point. I'm sorry to hear his condition is worsening, but he's talking to you, not me. You've seen him, not me. All he's given me is some letters with lame, half-ass apologizes for all the mess he's left me to deal with."

I crossed my arms. "So, what do you want me to do? Because I am still trying to figure out how to stay somewhat put together so that I don't fall completely apart."

Her shoulders buckled. "This is hard for me too. He's my brother," she said, quietly, her eyes downcast.

Zamir stood. "I'll go and leave you two to talk."

"Sit," I said, firmly. "We have business to discuss." I didn't take my eyes off Gabriella. He slipped back into his side of the booth without saying a word.

I stood, facing Gabriella. Softening, I reached for her hand, gently taking it into mine. "Look, I love Gable, and I want him to be well, but I still don't know what his recovery would mean for him and me."

She nodded, tears welling in her eyes. I was surprised there was no moisture in mine to match. I think I was all cried out.

Dark clouds lined the sky, signaling rain was coming. Sitting at my desk, I stared out of the window of my office. There was no blue sky in sight. The overcast was a perfect match for the somberness looming over me. I was thankful for the hour I had after leaving the café to decompress. The truths Zamir had unveiled had sent me reeling. Then there was Gabriella's unexpected popup, bringing more weight to the table.

I couldn't wait until my next therapy session. My baggage just kept getting heavier and harder to carry. I had a lot to unpack with Dr. Butler, but for now, I needed to focus on work. Soon, I would be meeting Zamir, his estranged wife, and her attorney for mediation.

This was supposed to be quick and to the point. They were on the same page for the financials, but the parenting plan had been challenging for them to agree on.

Zamir remained steadfast about what he wanted with very little flexibility on the custody agreement. I just prayed this mediation went well. My stomach had been in a ball of knots since this morning. The sooner they reached an agreement, the sooner this business between Zamir and I could be over, and hopefully we could just focus on rebuilding our friendship.

Seven years ago, I would have thought that Zamir and I would never be friends again. It felt good having him around. I realized now how much I'd missed our friendship.

Before we parted ways at the café that morning, I had agreed to his invitation to grab dinner later to catch up some more.

After Gabriella left, he probed a little about what was happening with Gable. I dismissed his inquisitiveness. He said he understood and dropped it. I was not ready to discuss the details of my marriage with him.

"Mrs. Rivers-Whitmore?"

"Yes, Fallon."

"Mr. Collins is here for your meeting."

"OK. Has the other party arrived as well?

"No. Not yet."

"You can send Mr. Collins to my office. When the other party arrives, show them to the conference room and notify me that they're here, please."

"You got it, boss." Her perky tone spread a small ray of sunshine my way, lifting my mood subtly.

A few seconds later, Zamir waltzed into my office, closing the door behind him. My eyes roamed up and down his strong but gentle build as he moved into the room with quiet confidence. The maroon button-down dress shirt he wore clung against his toned chest in an undeniably beautiful way. A roguish grin played on his face.

"The beautiful lady wanted me all alone, huh?" he teased, sinking into the chair in front of my desk.

My cheeks warmed with a blush. I giggled. "Whatever, silly." Straightening my posture, I opened the folder in front of me. "I want to go over my notes with you before the meeting just to confirm everything remains the same. Due to the unexpected interruption, we didn't get around to this earlier today."

I glanced up at him, catching a flicker of empathy in his gaze.

He nodded, waiting for me to continue.

I sighed deeply, sat back in my chair, and locked my hands together.

His brow quirked. "What is it?" he asked.

I shook my head. "Don't do that."

"Do what?" He leaned forward.

"Feel sorry for me."

Shoulders sagging, his attention momentarily slid from me and out the window as he smoothed his neatly trimmed goatee. I quietly studied him as his face shifted into the recognizable countenance he wore when he was deep in thought. Getting up from the chair, he turned back to me. His eyes bore into mine. He walked around the desk, never losing my gaze. Holding his hand out toward me, he gave me a knowing look. Without pause, I stretched my hand toward him, letting him take it into his.

He pulled me up and close to him until we stood barely an inch apart. "I don't feel sorry for you," he whispered. "I feel for you."

Closing my eyes, I swallowed hard, trying to push down the raw emotions that sprang up from my core as the heat radiating from his body slowly began melting away my rationale, leaving me torn between sense and sensibility.

In an instant, he released my hand. I opened my eyes and watched him move back to his chair.

"Back to those notes," he said, with a smile that barely reached his eyes.

Frozen in place, I stared at him, my legs like jelly. I shook my head in confusion, willing my brain back in control of my body and lowered into my chair. Clearing my throat, I picked up my pen and glanced over my notes. "You want half the week, every other weekend, and rotating holidays, correct?" I asked, my eyes lingering on the papers in front of me.

"Correct."

Looking up at him, my brow lifted. "What does she want?"

"She wants rotating weeks and rotating holidays, except Christmas. She wants us to split the day on Christmas."

"And that doesn't work for you?"

"No. What if I want to take him on a trip for Christmas?"

I gave an understanding nod.

I leaned forward. "Are you willing to compromise?"

"How so?" Mirroring me, he leaned forward too.

"You give her every other week. You already mostly agree on rotating holidays. Ask her for Christmas to be added to that rotation in exchange, that's if this can work for you."

He looked away. Staring out of the window again as if his thoughts were lost in the clouds, he leaned back. Moving his pursed lips from side to side, he leaned forward, resting his elbows on his legs, his chin settled onto the back of his hands. I knew him well. He needed uninterrupted time to think. I sat patiently as he turned every word I'd just said over in his head, along with several different scenarios he'd already thought of.

Turning his head back in my direction, he straightened, a wide grin spreading across his face. "Alright. Let's do it."

"Hold on now." I lifted a hand. "Your wife—"

"Ex-wife," he corrected.

Shaking my head, I rolled my eyes, playfully. "Your soon-to-be ex-wife is not here yet."

I glanced at the clock on the wall. It was fifteen minutes past the time the meeting should have started. "Is she always late?"

He frowned, reaching into his pocket to retrieve his phone. "Not normally. She hates being late." After a few swipes and taps, his brows drew together in concern.

"She's called and texted me. I turned my phone on silent when I first got here." He tapped the screen again, then paused to read her message.

He flew up from the chair. "I have to go." Fear flared in his eyes.

I stood. "Wait," I called out without moving from around my desk. "Zamir, what's wrong?" He had moved to the door.

"My son has been rushed to the emergency room again." His words quick and urgent. "I'm sorry. I'll call you to reschedule."

And just like that, he was gone.

I flopped back into my chair. When I ran into Zamir at the emergency room the night I went to see Brave, he told me his son was there, but was this a reoccurring thing? He never mentioned to me that his child was sick. Come to think of it, he never mentioned much about his child to me at all throughout this entire divorce process.

I wondered what made Zamir decide to have a child. One of the things about us that worked was we were both okay with not having children. We'd talked about what we wanted our future to look like during our senior year in high school.

There were many late-night phone conversations and just the two of us hiding out on the beach watching the sunset, talking about our career and family goals. He joked about how he would become a godparent someday, how he'd spoil his godchildren and then send them home to their parents.

At that time, I never imagined that we would become anything more than friends. It wasn't until college that I succumbed to my feelings for him, admitting to myself that I was in love with him.

Floating down memory lane, our first kiss replayed in my mind.

We were at a frat party that neither of us was enjoying. Aurora had suckered me into going with her, using her famous YOLO, line.

Already dressed for the party, she'd urged me to join her.

"Girl, you only live once." She'd closed my textbook and snatched my study guide from my fingers. "You've been studying non-stop since last night. You need a break."

I looked up, scowling at her. But I couldn't help but notice how gorgeous my friend looked. She was wearing a red mini bodycon dress that hugged her generously shaped behind.

The short dress had left most of her cocoa skin exposed, glistening from her favorite glitter body butter under the soft light. Her outfit choice was complemented by her crinkled micro locs, which hung half down in the back with the front pulled atop her head in a messy bun.

Still sitting, I reached to snatch my study guide back from her. She held it over her head.

"Ro, give me back my paper. I have an exam next Wednesday. I need to study. Besides, frat parties aren't my thing."

"Oh, come on Blou," she pleaded. "If you go, I promise to help you study tomorrow."

"Girl, what?" I'd cackled hard at her offer. "Now you know every time you go to a party you get drunk and have a hangover the next day."

Crossing her arms over her chest, she sucked her teeth and rolled her eyes. "Not every time. For real, girl, I got you."

I glared at her, mulling the invite over.

"Oouuu, you get on my nerves. Give me an hour to shower and get dressed."

A wide grin spread across her face. "Yay! I'll wait while you get dressed."

We'd walked into the party an hour and a half later. Aurora had immediately hit the spot reserved as a dance floor, joining the crowd that was already twerking and gyrating to a song from Cash Money Records by Juvenile, featuring Lil Wayne and Mannie Fresh. I grabbed a bottle of water from a cooler and retreated to a cozy corner.

I checked my phone, noticing a text from Brave—a picture of him in the hallway at his middle school throwing up the peace sign with a silly grin on his face. I rolled my eyes and slid the phone back into my clutch purse.

"I'm surprised to see you here."

I looked up to see Zamir standing over me. Feigning offense, I gasped and rested my hand on my chest.

"What? I get out sometimes."

He smirked. "You don't want to be here anymore than I do."

"Well, who drug you out?" I asked

"Mike."

"The things we do for our friends," I said with a half-smile.

"Come on. Let's get out of here."

I frowned. "And go where?"

He reached for my hand, gently pulling me from the chair. "You'll see."

He wore the same roguish grin that lit his beautiful face whenever he swept me from our high school hallway on occasion.

On one of our escapisms, he confided in me the reason he came to live with his father full-time. His mother's battle with alcohol had landed her in an inpatient rehabilitation center. It would often be the day after speaking to his mom that he would whisk me off.

We would spend our last class period in a park, sitting on the beach, or grabbing a bite to eat from a nearby food truck, chasing a moment of refuge before we had to return home.

At first, I didn't realize I needed these retreats as much as he did. Neither of our home lives were horrible, but they both carried realities that weighed heavier than we could admit.

This familiar gesture stirred a strong reminiscence that warmed my body from heart to toe. He walked me to his car and opened the door for me. Before sliding inside, I shot him a look that warned, *I better not regret this*. He responded with that affable smirk he gave when he wanted me to trust him without asking questions.

Our first stop was at a nearby sandwich shop. We rushed in ten minutes before closing and ordered two medium Philly cheese steak subs.

Soon after leaving the sandwich shop, we pulled over by at a waterfront park, which was mostly settled and quiet since the late hour.

Gathering our sandwiches, we got out and made our way to one of the benches near the water. We ate in silence, taking in the quietness around us. After finishing our sandwiches, we washed them down with the root beers we grabbed from the sandwich shop. Zamir had slid closer, turning to face me. Gently taking my hand in his, he locked eyes with mine.

"Thank you for being a great friend when I needed one the most," he said quietly. I searched his eyes. A gentle longing stared back at me, mirroring my own. His desire for me was no secret. Since our first year in college, he had continued to drop subtle hints that his feelings for me had grown far beyond platonic.

I wondered if my quiet yearning for him had now flickered visibly through my dreamy gaze. The softness of the park's lighting had made it possible for him to find my lips as he leaned in and kissed me softly, as if he'd always known.

Looping my hands around the back of his head, I pulled him in closer, kissing him back. He pulled my bottom lip into his mouth, sucking it gently. A low, soft moan had made its way up my throat as he pushed his tongue between my lips, deep and passionately. He groaned, pulling back slowly. With his eyes closed and his forehead resting against mine, he whispered, "We should go before things go too far."

I frowned, a warmth of disappointment and rejection spreading through my body. Catching my expression, he quickly shook his head.

"No, don't think I don't want you." He tilted my chin gently, drawing my gaze toward him. "I want to properly date you first. If you'll let me." He paused, letting his request float between us. "We've been in college for two years, and you've been turning me down since high school. Let me have you. Please."

Squeezing my legs together, I swallowed the moan that threatened to reveal that the sexy rasp in his plea had me shook between my thighs. He still wanted me. Relief flickered through me. I smiled and nodded. Slipping his hand into mine, he stood, taking me with him.

We stood still, quietly staying in that moment for a while, enthralled in each other's presence and oblivious to everything around us—except for the quiet rustle of the trees stirred by a soft breeze.

We had already been glued together as friends, but from that moment on, we were one—until life and hard decisions shifted our worlds apart.

Chapter *sixteen*

Me: *Hey, Zamir. How is your son?*

Zamir: *Pretty good. The first few days were a little rough, but he's doing much better. He'll be here for a few more days for observation.*

Me: *OK. I'm praying for him. I am here if you need to talk.*

Zamir: *Thank you. How are you feeling?*

Me: *I'm feeling OK. Thanks for asking. I'm about to head over to Aunt Gina's and Uncle Lance's for a cookout.*

Zamir: *Cool. Sounds fun. And hey, Esa and I discussed the options you suggested. We did come to a compromise, so thank you.*

Me: *That's great. So, no mediation then?*

Zamir: *Nope. All is well.*

Me: *Alrighty. I'll update the paperwork with those terms. Would you like to pick up the papers and have her sign, or will you both meet at my office to sign them?*

Zamir: *We'll meet at your office once Amir is home from the hospital and settled in. Could you pencil us in for this coming Tuesday at noon, please?*

Me: *Got it! Normally, you would need to go through Fallon to schedule, so you owe me for this special treatment, Mr. Collins. *Wink emoji**

Zamir: **Raised eyebrow emoji* Mm. What can I do to repay you for this "special treatment?"*

Me: *Mm. Let's see. *Thinking emoji* You can take an old friend to dinner.*

Zamir: *Oh, so you want a date? *Raised eyebrow emoji**

Me: **Eye roll emoji* Not quite. Just two friends having dinner.*

Zamir: *Deal. *Wink emoji**

Me: *We'll talk soon. Take care of your baby.*

Zamir: *Always do. And thank you, again, Blou Skies. You take care of YOU. *Wink emoji**

Tossing the phone in my tote of choice for the day, I threw it over my shoulder and headed to the kitchen to grab a bottle of water before moving to the front door. I opened it, stunned to see Gabriella standing there, finger raised to ring the doorbell.

Tilting my head, I frowned. "Gabriella. What are you doing here?"

"I'm sorry for popping up unannounced," she said, an unreadable expression etched across her face. "I wanted to tell you face-to-face."

"Tell me what?" I asked, stepping outside and gently closing the door behind me.

"Gable wants to see you."

I froze, dumbfounded. "What?"

"He said he called you a couple of times but didn't get an answer. He knows you don't answer unknown numbers but took a chance anyway. He asked if I'd tell you that he wants to see you."

"Gabriella, you told me that he can't have visitors while he in this trial."

"I also told you I went to see him, but you never let me explain how I was able to do so."

I crossed my arms, irritation bubbling up. "Explain, please." I struggled to keep the edge out of my tone.

"I was able to see him because he had been given his last round of treatments. Now it's just a waiting game. Either he's going to get better or worse."

"Why does he suddenly want me to come see him? I thought he didn't think I could handle seeing another person I love going through a sickness," I snapped, eyes narrowing.

"Right now, the treatments don't seem to be working, so he wants to see you while he's still alert." Her voice wavered. "Just in case."

Her fingers tightly clutched the straps of her purse as if the squeezing would keep the tears that welled in her eyes from falling.

My gaze drifted away from her. "When?" I asked, my clenched jaw beginning to soften.

"They've moved him to a facility in Florida, about an hour's drive from Parksdale," she said, her gaze lingering on my face, studying me, like she was trying to pinpoint which emotion I was feeling. "You can go any Monday, Wednesday, or Saturday."

This sounds like some type of prison visitation schedule, I thought, but I wouldn't dare say it out loud to Gabriella.

With a heavy sigh, I shifted my key from one hand to the other. "Can you text me the information, please—the hours and location? I need to get going."

She nodded. "Sure."

We walked together down the walkway toward the driveway. My car was outside the garage since my mobile detail appointment was that morning. As I approached it, I admired the flawless shine gleaming on the clean black exterior, courtesy of the fresh wax. Its sleek exterior, and polished armor, reflected a version of my life the world might imagine. But in reality, it was the antithesis of what my life really was right now.

"Gabriella," I called to her as she approached her own spotless ride, fishing through her purse for her key fob.

She turned to look at me but remained silent.

"Did you tell him?" I gave her a pointed look. "About what you saw at the café?"

Her eyes drifted briefly before settling them back on mine. She nodded, a speck of sadness in her gaze.

I returned a quick nod of understanding before slipping into the car, starting the engine and pulling out of the driveway, leaving my sister-in-law still fumbling for her key fob.

About thirty minutes later, I pulled into Aunt Gina's and Uncle Lance's driveway. From the looks of it, I was the first to arrive. Knowing Aunt Gina, she had probably only invited a few people from her church.

Brave's car was parked in the driveway and had been since Uncle Lance brought it there while Brave was in the hospital.

I had already braced myself for a conversation with Brave. I still didn't have the emotional bandwidth to unpack our drama right now, but I knew there was no avoiding it with us both being here today. So, on the ride over, I refused to allow any headspace for Gable. My soul needed a moment of rest from chaos. I didn't want to think about anything—just clear my mind. I cranked up my old school R&B playlist and belted the lyrics at the top of my lungs, distracting me from the anxiety that had been clawing at me since Gabriella showed up on my doorstep delivering the next bomb. Every time Gable's request that I come see him popped into my mind, I banished the thought. I didn't know what to think of that, but I couldn't think of it now.

Just as I was about to get out of the car, my phone flashed with a video call from Neveah.

"What's up, chica?" I answered.

She was wearing a black satin robe, her face softly touched with makeup. Peeping at her background, I knew she was sitting in her bedroom. "Are you at Aunt G's yet? she asked.

"Yup. Just got here."

"OK. I just have to slip my clothes on, and I'll be on my way in about an hour. But girl, I couldn't wait to tell you this." She leaned into the phone, lowering her voice.

Mirroring her, I leaned into the phone and whispered, "What?"

She laughed. "Why the heck are you whispering?"

"I mean, you're talking all quiet, so I'm just following your lead." I shrugged.

"Lukas is here. That's why I am talking low. He's in the shower, but I have my earpiece in so he can't hear you." She propped the phone up on her nightstand and picked up a purple sundress from the bed.

"Girl, you know you love purple." I chuckled.

"Ma'am, focus. Let me tell you before he comes out." She turned back toward the phone, leaning in again. "Guess who I met last night?"

Lifting an eyebrow, I leaned in farther. "Who?"

"Lukas's ex-wife," she whispered.

My eyes widened. "For real? And what happened? What do you think? Wait." I frowned. "How?" I thought you weren't ready for that."

"Everything went well. I'll fill you in later." She straightened, letting her robe fall and pulling on her dress. "I heard the shower turn off so, I'll talk to you later," she rushed. "Be there soon. Bye."

I shook my head as the call dropped. Grabbing my tote, and a book I'd been reading off the seat, I climbed out of the car and walked around to the back of the house. I knew Uncle Lance would be outside on the grill.

"Hey, Unc," I greeted.

"Hey, Blou Bear!" He wrapped his arms around me in a tight embrace.

"It's smelling good out here. What all you got there?"

He chuckled, knowing how much I loved his barbecue. We all did.

"Chicken, burgers, hotdogs, bratwurst, and of course, the best ribs in town." He winked. "I'm going to throw some salmon and veggies on here too."

"*Umm*. Sounds good," I said, rubbing my belly. "I came with an appetite." We both laughed.

"Aunt Gina must be in the kitchen working on the sides and dessert." I looked toward the back door leading directly into the kitchen.

"You know it." He placed some chicken wings in an aluminum pan. Glancing over at me, he sat it down off to the side of the grill.

He glanced at the book in my hand. "What's that you reading?"

"It's called The Love Songs of WEB Dubois."

"Ah. Ok. It's quite a big book, but you've always been a book worm."

I laughed. "Yes. It's pretty thick. I am half-way finished and it's fascinating. I'll tell you all about it when I'm done, Unc."

He smiled. "OK, darling. I can't wait to hear all about it." A soft but serious look crossed his face. "On another note, are you going to talk to your brother?" he asked, as he turned the chicken legs.

Biting my bottom lip, I kept my eyes on the sizzling meat as he flipped them one by one. "I actually would be OK if I never talked to him again, if I'm being honest."

Placing the tongs down, he closed the grill top over the meat and turned to look at me.

"Blou Bear," he said softly, "Brave told me and Gina what happened."

I crossed my arms, sliding my gaze anywhere else other than on Uncle Lance to avoid rolling them. We'd always been able to say what we felt to our parents and our aunt and uncle, but disrespect was never tolerated, no matter how old we got.

They had always been soft on Brave, but I don't care what he told them. He didn't do as I said, and even though all I had was just an ounce of trust for him, I trusted him, nonetheless. He should have listened to me and followed my guidance.

"I know that look. You can be just as stubborn as your father was." He chuckled. "Just hear him out, sweetheart."

"Uncle Lance," I said, locking eyes with him, "I told him to wait—not to do anything. Just wait on me to get an attorney at my firm to look over the contract." Heat surged inside of me just from talking about this with Uncle Lance. I was definitely not ready to talk to Brave.

"From the looks of it, he didn't do that." My voice elevated slightly.

His eyebrows raised. "Oh, you're calling me Uncle Lance instead of Unc. You must be some kind of upset with me." He laughed again.

Releasing a deep sigh, my shoulders relaxed. "I'm not upset with you. It's this situation." I glanced away, taking a deep breath. "I never should have helped him."

Uncle Lance placed a gentle hand on my shoulder. "Just hear him out. Please."

Looking him in his tired eyes, I sighed heavily. "OK. OK." I tipped
up on my toes and planted a kiss on his cheek. "I'm going to see what Aunt Gina is up to. Do you need anything from inside?"

"No, thank you, sweetheart." He pulled a rag from his pocket and wiped sweat from his forehead. "I have everything I need right now."

It was not quite summer yet, but a spring day in South Florida could easily be hot and humid. Although the weather was nice and not at its hottest, I still worried that Uncle Lance had not drank enough water.

"I'll bring you some water, Unc," I said, walking toward the back door.

When I entered the kitchen, it was empty. I didn't know where Aunt Gina was, but those sweet potato pies she had left cooling on the counter smelled and looked delicious. I peeked at the other pies. Some looked like they might be blueberry and apple. My stomach growled.

I grabbed a bottle of cold water from the refrigerator, took it outside to Uncle Lance, and returned inside just as Brave limped in on his crutches.

We both paused, catching each other's gaze.

"Hey," he greeted me. His eyes slid past me, landing on the pies.

"Hey," I said, looking away too. I walked over to the refrigerator and grabbed another bottle of water for myself.

"You mind grabbing me one too?"

I grabbed another bottle before turning and letting the door close behind me.

Handing him the water, I scanned the signed cast wrapped around his leg. I snickered before turning and taking a seat at the rustic walnut dining table. He was so childish. What grown man had people sign his cast?

He took a few hops toward the table before taking a seat across from me.

Twisting the top off the bottle, I relaxed back into the firm but comfortable cushion of the chair and took a long gulp of water. I didn't realize how thirsty I was until the water slid down my throat like a cool stream, refreshing my parched insides.

I felt Brave's stare as I read the words across the bottle wrapper, avoiding his eyes and the difficult conversation that I knew was coming. The water bottle had become a calming safety net for both me and him. Me because scanning the words kept me grounded and for him because as long as I was grounded, he was spared my wrath.

"Blou."

I glanced up at him and then back at the bottle, re-reading the label as if the words had changed.

"I know you're upset with me, but I want to explain what happened."

Taking my eyes from the safety of the bottle, I glared at him with an icy stare cold enough to freeze him in place.

My body grew hot as anger consumed me, joining forces with the mental exhaustion that had been constantly building for weeks. The rhythm of my heart drummed rapidly against my chest as my gut churned from anxiety.

"Upset is an understatement, Brave. I knew I shouldn't have trusted you." Before I could stop myself, the words crashed out, all rationale sank beneath the weight of my anger.

I slammed the water bottle on the table and lit into my little brother. "You know what? This is really on me. It's on me because I'm the real problem. I keep giving you chance after chance knowing you don't do anything right. It's my own error in judgement, thinking you can handle carrying out a plan of that magnitude on your own." Every word I spoke wreaked of disgust, the tension in my twisted expression bearing no mercy. "You," I spat, pointing at him, "you are always messing up."

Hurt flickered in his eyes. "You don't even know what happened." His eyes cast down toward the table, resting his gaze on his intertwined hands.

I glared at him, wanting him to look in my eyes and face my wrath. "I don't need to know the details just to know whatever happened is on you."

"Yeah, of course. No matter what the truth is, I will always be a huge disappointment to you, big sis." *Big sis* fell from his lips like a nasty word. He looked up, finally meeting my gaze. "Who can compare to your perfect life, right?" Sarcasm thickened his tone.

"*Tuh.*" I rolled my eyes. "My life is not perfect. I never claimed it to be. You don't know the half of what I am going through right now." Tears pricked the corners of my eyes. I blinked to keep them from falling.

"Maybe because you never let me in."

"Maybe because you have been nothing but a thorn in my side ever since you got here," I shot back.

Brave's eyebrows furrowed. His eyes flashed with something unrecognizable. Confusion. Pain. Maybe both.

"Since I got here?"

"Yes. Since you got here," I snapped, my voice rising. "If it weren't for you, my mother would—"

"*Our* mother," he cut in, his voice cracking but quiet.

"What?" I gave him an incredulous look.

"She was our mother." This time he spoke a little louder, a little firmer. "Not just yours, Blou. I lost my mother too."

Leaning in, I glared at him with fire behind my eyes. The heat inside me intensified. "You didn't know her," I retorted.

Brave slowly straightened, careful not to hit his extended leg against the table. His crutch that once rested against his body slid down and clanked against the mahogany hardwood floor. Ignoring the thud of the crutch, our gazes both fierce and unrelenting locked in place. His jaw pulled together tightly matching the clench of my own.

"That's the thing, Blou," he said, his tone steady. "I understand how painful it is for you that you lost our mother, but you—" He paused, pressing his teeth gently against his bottom lip. His face softened slightly. "You experienced her smell, her touch, her love." A single tear released from the corner of his eye and slid down his cheek. "You have memories to hold on to. You had the pleasure of knowing her."

The tears filling his eyes and the pain in his voice caught me off guard. I was the one who was supposed to be hurt, the one who grieved for my mother daily since her unexpected death.

In a session with Dr. Butler, she said that Brave didn't need to know her to grieve her absence, but I brushed that rationalization off. I had found it hard to believe when she said it.

Softening just a little, I crossed my arms over my chest. "I didn't think you cared much because she never even held you. You never felt her touch."

Brave shook his head in disbelief. "How could you say that?" His tone was slightly sharp. "Why do you think I went to therapy in the first place?"

I shrugged, glancing away.

He extended his arm out. "Why do you think I wear this?" He snapped the rubber band against his wrist. "To distract me if the panic attacks come back. Geesh, Blou." Lowering his face in his hands, he blew out a long breath. "I have had nothing but a constant reminder that my birth is what killed her." Looking up toward me, he wiped away tears. Our eyes met, as I blinked back my own. "And not just because she isn't here, but also because your coldness toward me won't let me forget it."

"But she would still be here if—"

"If what?" He threw his hands up in defeat. "If I had never been born? Well, big sis, I spent years blaming myself too and after countless therapy sessions, I have come to terms with the fact that our mother's death was not *my* fault. I didn't ask to be here."

I gazed at my little brother, studying his strained face and tense posture. Brave was right. Aunt Gina and Neveah were right. Dr. Butler was right. They were all right. Our mother's death was not Brave's fault. But I needed someone—something—to blame. I suddenly realized, that is the only thing that seemed to hold me together all these years—blame.

As silence stretched between us, tension slowly melted away, leaving fresh air to breathe. Glancing over Brave's head, I noticed Aunt Gina standing in the arched entrance to the kitchen. She quietly moved toward us. The flood gate of tears that I had been willing to stay back flowed freely from my eyes. Placing my elbows on the table, I buried my face in my hands and sobbed.

Aunt Gina rested a gentle hand on my shoulder.

"Blou, honey, it's OK. Let it all out." Her soft voice filled with compassion flowed through my ears, finding its way to my heart. Her gentle comfort always reminded me so much of my mother's tender spirit.

Raising my head, I looked across the table at Brave. The bleakness in his eyes reflected a myriad of emotions that I couldn't name but only feel—a mirror of my own pain that I'd carried for so many years.

Aunt Gina moved closer and slowly lowered into the chair next to me and Brave. One of her hands found mine as she reached for Brave's hand with the other.

"I've been waiting so long for the two of you to have this conversation." She looked from Brave to me. "Holding on to unforgiveness and bitterness is never good for anybody. I don't care how good your life looks on the outside, you'll never have true peace and happiness until you release all that junk from inside of you."

Slowly nodding my head, I gently squeezed Aunt Gina's hand.

"Now your mother…" She paused, glancing at Brave and then back at me. "She knew she was taking a risk by carrying Brave."

My brows creased. "What are you talking about Aunt Gina?" I asked, my eyes resting intently on her.

"When Cecily found out she was pregnant with your brother, the doctors told her that if she didn't terminate the pregnancy, she was putting her life at risk. But your mother was strong headed—a lot like you." She nodded in my direction. "She said there was no way she was killing her baby and that she would just have to leave her life in God's hands."

Shaking my head, I swallowed a lump that was forming in my throat. "Aunt Gina, you never told me this before. Neither did dad. He was OK with her decision?"

I glanced at Brave. He sat quietly but looked just as stunned as I was. This new information landed hard in my stomach causing somersaults and a touch of nausea.

Aunt Gina tilted her head, holding my gaze. "He let that be up to your mother. They both knew after the complications she had while delivering you—to have another baby was not advised by the doctors. Your father supported her decision, never giving any of his own thoughts about what she chose to do with her body."

I blinked slowly. Baffled, my eyes darted between Brave and Aunt Gina. "Complications delivering me?"

Her lips pursed into an empathic line, eyes brimming with soft sorrow. "Yes, sweetheart. There were complications during your delivery too." Releasing our hands, Aunt Gina pushed up from the chair. "I'll be right back. I have something for you."

Perplexity shook the foundation of what I thought I understood about my birth. Everything I had assumed. Nowhere in any of the stories my parents told me about the day I was born did they mention complications.

A wave of emotions washed over me. My mother could have died giving birth to me, and I would have never known her at all. Here I was blaming Brave all these years, and I could have been standing in his shoes, except I would have been the only child. The weight of this new reality rested heavily on my chest. Closing my eyes, I slowed my breathing. *Inhale. One, two, three, four. Hold. One, two, three, four, five, six, seven. Exhale. One, two, three, four. Inhale. One, two...*

"Are you OK?" Brave interrupted, his voice just above a whisper.

I nodded. When I heard Aunt Gina's footsteps, I opened my eyes, releasing the tears that rested behind them.

She returned with a notebook. "This is a journal your mother kept about both her pregnancies and your birth."

Shock rendered me speechless as she handed it to me. I ran my hand over the soft dark brown leather notebook. I'd seen my mother write in this journal a few times but I hadn't thought of it after her death. I had no idea Aunt Gina had held on to something of my mother's that was so personal—so sacred.

I looked up at Brave noticing his misted eyes resting on the book.

She turned to Brave. "It might be helpful for you to read some of it too." She lowered back into the chair. "One thing I do know is your father loved you unconditionally no matter what, and so did your mother—she loved you before she ever saw you," she said, gently squeezing Brave's hand. "Your father didn't want you two to know any of this until you were ready to hear it, and I think it's time."

She pressed her lips into a tight smile. "I've watched you your whole lives. It's been a struggle, but now you two are at a crossroad in your relationship with each other. You're still trying to find your way, but you're healing. I can see your growth."

She leaned in and gently patted both our hands. "Therapy has never been my thing or something I ever even thought about trying. I leans on the Lord Jesus, and the Lord Jesus only." She chuckled. "But I must admit that it seems to be working for the two of you."

Wiping tears from my face, I couldn't help but giggle. Aunt Gina was the true definition of an old-school Christian.

"You can have Jesus and therapy too, Aunt Gina." I winked.

She shook her head, a small smile playing on her lips. "To each their own, sweetheart." Giving my hand a quick, gentle pat, she slowly rose from the chair. One brow lifted, she nodded in my direction. "Now, you hear your brother out about that crypto stuff. This tension between the two of you has been going on long enough. I'm going to go check on your uncle—make sure he's been drinking enough water. Y'all know how hardheaded that man can be."

Brave and I exchanged a knowing look. We did know.

Before going out the back door, Aunt Gina stopped and turned back. "Blou?"

"Ma'am," I answered, turning toward her. A puzzled look lit her face. "Where in the world is Gable?"

Chapter *seventeen*

"So, I had to explain to Aunt Gina where Gable is after hearing Brave out about how he ended up in the mess he's in."

Zamir and I were tucked away at a booth in the back of a steakhouse he'd suggested we go to for dinner. I had filled him in on everything going on except the details of the baby situation. I told him I found out Gable had been keeping secrets that I wasn't ready to share. It was shameful enough to reveal that part of my life to my family just the day before.

"Wow. Yesterday was a long day for you." He reached over and gently laid his hand over mine.

Releasing a deep sigh, I took a small sip of an expensive wine, which he had insisted I try. The smooth, semi-dry, fruity aftertaste warmed my insides, melting away the tension I'd been carrying since the day I left my aunt and uncle's house.

Aunt Gina and Uncle Lance had both been comforting support as I laid out everything about Gable, from the sickness to the baby, to him now requesting to see me. At first, I worried about how they would react—if they would pressure me to go talk to him. To decide right away whether to stay married or leave. But I should have known they would be a safe place to land. They always had been.

Aunt Gina's words still rang fresh in my ears. *"Sweetheart, seems like you are tethering on the edge of grace. You have plenty of soul searching to do as you decide how much of it to give and how you're going to give it."* She patted my hand. *"And not just for others but for yourself too."*

Uncle Lance took both my hands in his. "Let us pray with you Blou Bear." I glanced at Brave sitting quietly across from me. He'd briefly caught my gaze before bowing his head and closing his eyes. I nodded at Uncle Lance and bowed my head.

"Earth to Blou." Zamir's voice and waving hand pulled me back from my aunt and uncle's living room just as the waiter approached.

"Refill on your water, ma'am?" he asked, calm but theatrical.

Glancing at my half-empty glass, I nodded. "Yes, please."

I looked over at Zamir as the waiter topped off my glass with bottled water. His soft eyes were fixed on me, as if he were trying to take back all the parts of me, he had let slip from his grasp almost eight years ago.

"Can I get you anything else?" the waiter asked.

"No thank you," we answered in unison.

The waiter nodded, gave a faint smile and walked away.

"Oh, before I forget," Zamir said, snapping his finger, "we need to push our meeting back one more time. Esa has an important work trip coming up and she leaves on Tuesday. Can we move it to the following Tuesday?"

"Sure. I will update Fallon." I smiled.

"Thank you." A smile played on his lips as his gaze deepened. "You haven't aged a bit since college."

"You haven't much either." I smirked. "The beard does add a couple of years, making you look, *um*, roughly, thirty-five years old instead of thirty-three."

He laughed. "You never could give a compliment without throwing some shade."

Laughing with him, I glanced down at my half-eaten medium-well steak, picked up the fork and knife, and carved off a small piece.

"At least you matured from ordering those well-done steaks," he teased.

I playfully rolled my eyes. "Shut up. I don't like blood running from anything I have to eat." I pointed at the small piece of medium rare wagyu he had left on his plate. "You just worry about your food."

He laughed again before leaning in. His expression shifted to more serious, concerned.

"So are you going to help Brave out of this situation since Tyrek scammed his way into the contract?"

Placing the fork down, I finished chewing and swallowed the savory piece of ribeye.

"I've been thinking about it since last night and all day." My jaws tightened. The tension that had been slowly dissipating inched back into my shoulders. "If I want to protect my investment—I mean, the money I put into his investment—then, of course."

He nodded. "I understand how you feel about him not waiting until you had the lawyer at your firm to look at the contract, but from what you've told me, he did get duped. I think his intentions were good."

Blowing out a deep breath, I settled back into the booth. "Yeah. It seems like he really thought letting Tyrek's lawyer review everything while I was out of town was the right thing to do." I raised a brow. "But I told him—I explicitly told him—I didn't want Tyrek involved at all."

"He must have really trusted his friend."

I gave him a knowing look. "Yes, he did. His so-called friend. But I never have. Brave knows that." Sitting up straighter, I locked eyes with Zamir. "I just hate that it took him getting manipulated and physically hurt for him to see what I've always seen."

"Yeah, I hate that for him," Zamir agreed. "Confronting Tyrek probably wasn't the best idea either, especially alone."

I shook my head. "Nope. Throwing a punch at Tyrek was reckless, especially with Tyrek's brother standing right there."

"Has Brave pressed charges against them for attacking him?" His brows furrowed, a spark of anger flashing in his eyes. "They could have killed him."

I leaned forward and took a sip of wine. "Brave says, since he barged in to their house and attacked Tyrek first, he's letting that go, but he wants him out of the contract."

Zamir picked up the Old-Fashioned he had been nursing for the last thirty minutes and took a small sip.

"It's messed up how Tyrek added that silent investor clause in the contract without Brave knowing, and that attorney should be disbarred."

My family had loved Zamir since they'd met him at the start of our high school senior year, and he had the same love for them.

His concern sent flutters to my stomach. I crossed my legs as a warmth pulsed between my thighs. Under the table, my raised foot tapped gently against Zamir's leg.

"Oops. Sorry." Our eyes met.

His gaze danced with a sparkle—reflecting something heated, a familiar yearning.

"No worries." He took my bare foot and rested it on his knee. "I see you still kick your shoes off everywhere you go." He smirked.

His hands caressed my foot in slow, soothing strokes. I rested my head back on the seat, releasing a soft, quiet moan. This foot massage reminded me that I was supposed to schedule a spa day with the girls. With everything going on, it had totally slipped my mind.

"You were saying?" A playful smile curved at the corners of his mouth.

I cleared my throat and continued.

"It's a matter of proving the attorney knew what Tyrek was up to. That's a whole other thing."

I reached for the ice water and took a sip, hoping to cool the fire rushing through my body as his soft hands stroked my aching foot.

"Brave should have re-read the copy of the contract Tyrek

handed him before signing it instead of assuming it was the exact contract they'd composed together. The copy he gave me raised some concerns, but nothing close to what Tyrek added in the new version. At least the vendors Tyrek introduced Brave to are legit."

I pulled my foot back from Zamir's grasp and straightened.

"Tyrek's spiel about the vendors threatening to pull out if he didn't close the deal by a certain time was just a ploy—a pressure tactic to get him to sign that bogus contract before I got back from DC."

"So, your main focus is to have the contract voided?" he asked. Curiosity glimmered in his eyes.

"That's one idea. *How* we're going to do that is a different story." I placed my elbows on the table and rested my chin against my hands. "I'll talk to Justin when I get into the office in the morning—see what can be done. But I think I know a way to get Tyrek to back out of the contract without taking this to court."

A comfortable silence fell between us. Our eyes lingered, revealing everything without any spoken words. The undeniable connection that had never wavered since the time we met at the movie theater pulled us in like a magnetic force.

The quiet hum of the restaurant dulled even more in the background as I fell deeper into his amorous stare.

"Have you all had a chance to look over the dessert menu?" The waiter's timing was both good and bad.

Without taking his eyes off me, Zamir answered, "I'm stuffed. I'll pass. Thank you."

"Same here." Releasing Zamir's gaze, I glanced up at the waiter.

"We'll take the check, please." Zamir gave the waiter a quick smile before resting his eyes back on me.

"Sure." The waiter returned the smile before he walked away.

Turning my attention back to Zamir, I relaxed into my seat. "Enough about me. What's up with you?" I said, slightly leaning my head to the side. "How's Amir doing?"

He exhaled. "He's doing better. I'm happy he's home from the hospital. He seems to be back to himself, but I know it's just a matter of time before—" He paused. Sadness filled his eyes.

I sat in silence, giving space for him to take the time he needed.

"I'm pretty sure he's going to need another blood transfusion soon." He shook his head. His eyes glistened. "The doctors have been trying to stabilize his condition for a few months. He was fine and suddenly, he just collapsed one day at school."

I reached out and took his hand in mine. It trembled slightly.

"I feel useless knowing there is nothing I can do to help. I can't even—" The words stuck in his throat. He closed his eyes, and I knew it was to stop the tears he held back from falling.

"If you don't mind me asking, what condition does he have?"

Opening his eyes, he gently squeezed my hand.

My phone rang, rousing us both from this somber yet intimate exchange.

I patted his hand before pulling back and reached inside my handbag to retrieve my phone.

It was Brave.

I decided I would call him back later. I didn't want to interrupt this moment with Zamir when he was letting me in after missing so much of his life—the life he had built without me. I was feeling the comfort of the bond we once shared, and I didn't want this moment to pass immaturely. I sent the call to voicemail and turned my attention back to Zamir.

The phone rang again. Brave. Again.

"I'm sorry. It's Brave blowing me up," I said softly, my finger lingering over the screen before answering the call. "Give me a second, please."

"Brave, this better be important," I hissed quietly into the phone.

Brave's words instantly turned my stomach into tight knots.

"OK. I'm on my way," I said, hurriedly, and disconnected the call.

I looked at Zamir. His brows etched with concern as he searched my panicked eyes for answers.

"Uncle Lance might have had a heart attack."

Chapter *eighteen*

"This is one reason I don't want children. People can be here to-day and gone tomorrow," I said, watching Dr. Butler's soft expression that revealed nothing but her attentiveness.

I paused, the weight of my words settling. "I can be here today and gone tomorrow, and then, who would my child have?"

Dr. Butler's voice came as gentle as her eyes. "Let me first say, I'm glad that your uncle is OK."

"Thank you. He's been following the doctor's orders daily, but it's only been a little over a week so, we'll see how long that lasts. Thankfully, it was only a false alarm—just chest pains from dehydration—but it was terrifying to think he might've had a heart attack."

"The scare with your uncle heightened your awareness of how quickly you can lose someone," she said. "That triggered the anxiety you feel about having children and potentially leaving them behind?"

"Well, yeah. I lost my parents at a young age." I shifted in my chaise, straightening. "I lost Zamir, not to death, but it felt like abandonment. Gable left me. He actually *did* abandonment me, then, he could possibly die. And his secrets…the secrets are another story. Brave could have been beaten to death, and what if

Uncle Lance had actually had a heart attack and died? I know death is inevitable but it's always seem to be so sudden or drastic."

Dr. Butler nodded slowly. "You've experienced a lot of loss—some through death, others through betrayal and abandonment," she said, her voice delicate and steady. "I don't know Gable's reasons for handling his illness the way that he did, but whatever they were, it's been incredibly difficult for you. From your perspective, it's another reminder that people you love don't stay. The recent trouble with Brave—a reminder that people close to you have let you down."

She leaned slightly, her eyes warm and grounded. "Like Zamir. Let's explore that a little more. Did you expect him to choose you instead of taking the job in DC?" She let the question linger, giving me space to sit with it.

I nodded slowly, the truth I'd buried pressed heavily on my chest. Tears pricked the corners of my eyes.

"When Zamir decided to stay in DC, I told myself it wasn't a big deal. If I could survive losing my parents, then I could survive losing him. I convinced myself that people leave me. That's just how my life is meant to be, so I decided to let go—to not love him anymore." I released a deep sigh.

"But you never stopped, did you?" she asked.

I slowly shook my head. "Now, he's popped back into my life after all this time. I doubt he'll stick around. Who knows? What if I allow him to get close to me again, and he transfers back up North? But the truth is, I've enjoyed his company, and that's scary." I paused. "Of course, we're only friends, and he doesn't owe me anything."

I wiped a single tear from my cheek. "When Gable and I got together, I waited for him to leave or die for years. Eventually, I started to believe that things could be different, that maybe I was wrong. Maybe he would stay. So, I started trusting that, and now, he's gone, and I don't know if he's coming back, which tells me I made the right decision by not having a child."

Blinking away more tears. I watched Dr. Butler's expression shift. Something close to empathy washed over her face. The, non-judgmental calmness in her demeanor silently reinforced the safety of the space she'd provided.

She spoke gently. "I wonder…is it truly the fear of leaving a child behind or the fear of being left again?"

She paused, letting the question settle.

I shifted again, relaxing further into the softness of the chaise. The soft hum of the air conditioning filled the silence between us, a gentle reminder that time doesn't stop even when my world pauses. To keep up, I had to stay moving.

"I guess it's both. My mother died having a child. Then, I found out that she almost died having me too. I lost my father. I can't imagine having children and then leaving them without parents. I know how that feels."

Dr. Butler's eyes softened further.

"The trauma of your mother's death, the loss of your father…they've shaped how you see love and safety." She paused, letting the hard truth land in the soft space between us. I hadn't read my mom's journal yet. I wasn't avoiding it. I just wanted to wait until I had less distractions—wait for the right time. But Dr. Butler's assessments made me wonder if reading them would bring more clarity and maybe even some closure.

"You've lived what it means to be a child left behind. And now you're trying to protect a child who doesn't exist from that same pain. That's compassion, Blou. That's love."

Her words gripped my chest, the ache sharper now with the shift in understanding.

"You've carried so much grief," she continued, her tone even more gentle than before. "It sounds like, for so long, you've felt you had to be strong, to quietly hold your pain. What would it mean to imagine a future where love doesn't always end in a tragic loss?"

I swallowed hard, her question echoing inside me—a future where love didn't always end in a tragic loss.

"I don't know what that looks like," I admitted, my voice barely above a whisper. "I've never seen that in my life."

She nodded, her expression still tender. "That makes sense.

When loss becomes familiar, having hope can feel unsafe. Think about how you and Zamir's relationship ended. It was painful, but do you do you see that as a tragic loss?

I looked down at my hands, noticing how tightly I held them together. Releasing them and letting my shoulders fall forward. I looked back at my therapist. Her gaze hadn't wandered. I mulled over her question. I had been so caught up in how traumatic all my losses had been, I never thought about it that way.

"Now that I think about it, I don't see our breakup as tragic. I see it as hurtful, a form of rejection and abandonment, but not necessarily a tragic loss. I also don't think I took the time to grieve that loss. I met Gable not long after and things between us progressed rather quickly."

"Um-hm. It sounds like you may have experienced love that hasn't ended tragically for you after all," she smiled and continued, "and, maybe, it's not about erasing your fear. Maybe it's about learning to live beside it. Letting love in anyway—taking the chances, despite the fear."

She leaned in slightly.

"I know it's terrifying because the outcome you desire isn't always guaranteed, but that's where healing begins." Smiling softly, her brow lifted. "And Blou, remember, grace. Give yourself grace."

I took in every word, exhaling slowly, sinking deeper into the cushion as if it could shield me from the heaviness of the truth, I had no choice but to face.

"You don't have to decide anything today," she added softly, "but maybe the question isn't whether you should have children. Maybe it's whether you believe you deserve a life where love stays—where you aren't always preparing to be left."

I nodded.

"I'd like you to take some time to process everything we just discussed over the next week." She smiled. "And if it's OK with you, I'd like you to journal. How does that sound?"

Returning the smile, I nodded again. "Of course. You know I love when you give me homework."

She chuckled.

"But, Dr. Butler," I said leaning in, "before we disconnect, I need to talk to you about my upcoming visit with Gable."

Chapter *nineteen*

I sat in the conference room at the law firm waiting for Zamir, Esa and her attorney to arrive. If nothing had changed on her end, this meeting should be short, quick, and procedural.

Still, I had been anxious all morning. Part of it was knowing that after this meeting, I'd be finally heading to see Gable. But mostly, I was about to come face-to-face with the woman my first love was divorcing, and I was his attorney.

I wondered if Zamir told her about me at any point in their relationship—if she knew his first love was advising him on their divorce.

I knew she didn't want the divorce, though she wasn't contesting it either. Zamir had said she did something unforgivable—something he didn't want to name and opted to go with irreconcilable differences as the reason for the divorce.

I didn't know what she had done exactly, that was serious enough for Zamir to file for a divorce, but I could only assume it was not a minor incident.

Then again, he once walked away from me without a fight, and I was the love of his life, so who knows.

During my entire relationship with Zamir, I was happy—head

over heels for him. His passion for me mirrored my feelings through his actions and words. We supported each other deeply. What we had worked. I hadn't imagined life without him until distance tested the fate of our relationship and won.

My thoughts drifted to the voice messages I had saved in my cloud storage.

I opened my laptop, pulled up my cloud account, and logged in.

I held my breath as I retrieved the messages, letting out a slow, intentional exhale as I clicked on the first one.

Message 1: *Blou, I think we should talk. I don't want to end things like this between us.*

Message 2: *Hey, Blou Skies. I miss you. I miss our friendship. Can we please talk?*

Message 3: *I know our breakup was hard for you. It's hard for me too, but I don't think we should shut each other out.*

Message 4: *I found a photo of us in one of my books. It was the one when we went to the spring fair and I won you that oversized stuffed elephant. I miss you. I hope we can talk soon.*

Message 5: *I went by your place, but you had already moved out. I just wanted to let you know that I'm moving. I'm being transferred to the Florida office. They've downsized the DC office, and the New York office didn't need me full-time.*

Message 6: *It's been about a month since I last called. I'm in Florida now and was hoping we could get together and talk. I miss you so much. I have been beating myself up for weeks because I can't believe I let the best part of my life walk away from me. Nothing has been the same without you. Please, call me. Talk to me.*

Message 7: *I've been leaving messages for several weeks—a few months. I don't know if you've listened, but this will be the last. I went by Aunt Gina's, looking for you. I met your husband. Seems like a good guy. I wish you all the happiness in the world. I will always love you, Blou Skies. Take care.*

Fallon stuck her head in the conference room just as the last message finished playing. I hadn't even noticed the tears that had slid down my cheeks.

"Blou, Mr. and—" She paused, stepping further inside. "Are you alright?" Concerned etched on her round reddish-brown face.

"Huh…I—" I reached for a Kleenex from the center of the table and lightly dabbed my face, drying the tears. "*Um*. Yeah. I'm good."

"Are you sure, boss?"

I forced a half smile. "Yes, Fallon. I'm fine. Thank you."

Fallon hesitated before asking, "Do you want me to send in Mr. and Mrs. Collins and her attorney?"

I ran my hand down the front of my soft pink pantsuit, pressing out invisible wrinkles, and straightened my posture.

"Yes. I'm ready." I nodded in her direction. "Send them in."

"OK," Fallon replied, still looking unsure of my readiness for this meeting. "I'll get them."

Esa and her attorney entered the room ahead of Zamir. Although I had never seen Esa before, I could easily distinguish her from her attorney.

My eyes glazed over the beautiful lady who appeared to match my five-six height as she sashayed deeper into the room to the side of the table opposite me. Her jet-black hair was neatly styled into Bantu knots at the crown, with loose curls cascading down her back and around her shoulders.

The wide-legged yellow jumpsuit she wore effortlessly complemented her velvety-brown skin. I couldn't deny, this good sis had it going on.

I stood and extended my hand to her. "Hi. I'm Blou Rivers-Whitmore, Zam…Mr. Collins's attorney." I smiled, meeting her eyes as she shook my hand.

She glanced at Zamir and then back to me, returning a kind but knowing smile. "I'm Esa—Esa Collins. It's nice to finally meet you."

Finally meet me? My stomach flipped. Did she know I was Zamir's ex?

I kept my expression smooth and unwavering as I turned to her attorney, offering her my hand.

With a firm shake, she introduced herself. "Zandra Newman. I am representing Mrs. Collins." Her smile was soft, professional.

I turned toward Zamir who had come to stand beside me. I quickly searched his eyes for a hint of what Esa's comment meant. His unreadable gaze met me with a slight curve of his lips, a smile that revealed nothing.

"Mr. Collins." I gave him a quick nod, then glanced across the table at Esa and Ms. Newman. "Please, have a seat," I gently instructed.

Opening the case file in front of me, I looked between Esa and her attorney. "If I understand correctly, Mrs. Collins, you and Mr. Collins have agreed to all the terms that are outlined in the divorce petition. Correct?"

Esa nodded in agreement. A tender sadness filled her misty eyes. She blinked quickly, burying the tears that threatened to fall. Her attorney's attention was fixed on me, waiting for me to proceed.

I turned my eyes on Zamir, signaling him to confirm.

"Yes," he replied, his tone steady. But his gaze flickered with a familiar ache. The same sadness I'd seen in his eyes during our final goodbye years ago, a few weeks after our breakup when we exchanged the belongings that had accumulated over the course of our relationship.

But this time, there was something else in his eyes—something I wasn't quite sure of. A hint of what I'd seen in his eyes just last night at dinner before Brave's call about Uncle Lance interrupted us.

"If there is nothing either of you wish to discuss further, we can move forward with signing the dissolution of marriage, and I'll file with the court tomorrow morning," I said, looking from one to the other.

I slid the divorce papers in front of Zamir and placed a pen on top.

He picked up the pen, took one last glance over each page, then began initialing and signing where required. Once finished, he placed the pen down and slid the papers back to me.

I handed them directly to Ms. Newman, catching a glimpse of Esa's regretful gaze piercing into Zamir whose eyes followed the official documentation that would unravel him from the woman he'd shared years of his life with.

Ms. Newman reviewed the decree, nodding to no one in particular.

"Everything looks the same as we discussed," she said, handing Esa a pen and sliding the papers toward her.

We waited as Esa scanned each page, her eyes moving slowly, deliberately.

The faint chatter of colleagues and their clients passing by the conference room mingled with the hush of our breathing, stretched a fragile quietness between us.

Zamir's message played back in my head. *I can't believe I let the best part of my life walk away from me.*

Under the table, I reached for Zamir's hand, giving it a gentle, comforting squeeze as Esa scribbled her signature on the final line, quietly declaring that their marriage was over.

Chapter *twenty*

"Are you sure you don't need us to go with you?" Neveah asked, concern flickering in her eyes.

"No. This is something I need to do alone." I placed the phone down on a shelf next to my perfumes and searched the color-coordinated hoodies lining my closet.

"I mean, we don't have to go in with you," Aurora chimed in, reappearing on the screen after putting us on hold for over five minutes. I'd almost forgotten she was still on the call.

"Yeah. We can wait in the car for moral support after you come out," Neveah co-signed, her voice softer now.

I grabbed a Power in Black hoodie I hadn't worn yet, pulled it over my head, and picked up the phone again.

"OK. I like that PIB hoodie," Aurora grinned. "Ms. Dark Choc-Lit." She snapped her fingers and swerved her head in a circle, reading the bold lettering across my chest.

I smiled into the camera. "Thank you, Ro. Just got it last week."

I propped the phone against a bottle of Fenty Beauty perfume so I could still see them while I slipped on a pair of jeans.

Neveah's brow furrowed. "I like that you're black and proud, sis."

She held her fist up in the black power sign. "So am I, but…you haven't seen your husband in over a month and you're wearing a hoodie and jeans?"

Aurora gasped, covering her mouth in mock surprise. "Not Ms. Positivity judging her outfit choices." She burst into laughter.

Neveah rolled her eyes, lips pursed. "Girl, I'm not judging. I'm just saying. You don't think you should wear something a little more…you know? Cute. Sexy."

Now it was my turn to roll my eyes. "Girl, what? Why?" I grimaced, nostrils flaring. "With everything he's put me through, I don't even know if I want him. I'm definitely not going out of my way to appease his lustful eyes."

They both laughed. "Appease his lustful eyes?" Aurora snickered. "That makes absolutely no sense in this situation. Besides, I honestly don't think a dying man cares what you're wearing."

Neveah and I both glared into our phones at Aurora.

Her eyes widened. "I'm sorry. Girl, I…Sorry." She winced.

"Ro, you don't know what the hell to say sometimes," Neveah scolded, her eyes narrowing, "or what not to say."

Aurora's shoulders sagged, her bottom lip jutting into a pout. "Yeah, that was my bad, Blou. That was insensitive."

I waved her off, sucking my teeth. "Girl, it's fine. The corners of my mouth lifted into a soft smile. "Unfortunately, that is a possibility. I've been preparing myself for whatever happens."

The girls' chat had shifted quickly—from hyping up my hoodie to death. Silence fell between us, soaking up the melancholy that had crept into our blissful conversation.

I cleared my throat, breaking the awkward lull. "Listen, I actually might need y'all to be there." My eyes shifted from one face to the other. "I don't know what to expect, so maybe I shouldn't drive myself."

They nodded in unison.

"OK, of course," Neveah said.

Aurora stood from where she'd been sitting. "I'll meet y'all at your house, Blou." She looked at her watch. "I gotta call the sitter right quick and have her pick up Layla from school."

Neveah nodded. "See y'all in twenty minutes then."

I nodded. "OK," I echoed quietly.

After disconnecting the call, I sat at the vanity tucked inside my closet and stared into the mirror. LED lights trimmed the frame, casting a luminous glow—the kind of glow I longed to feel on the inside again.

I studied my reflection, wondering how I got here. How had my seemingly close-to-perfect life come to blows with misery.

I fluffed my perfectly defined curls—the result of a successful twist out. Camille Rose's twisting butter snatches these 4B kinky curls together every time.

The Juvia's Place tan eye shadow I had smoothed over my eye lids before work this morning was still flawlessly intact.

I pulled open the top drawer of the vanity and retrieved a brown tinted lip gloss and dark brown liner. Leaning in closer to the mirror, I etched the liner along my lips, then glided the gloss over them. I pressed my lips together a couple of times, blending the two. Gazing at my reflection, I forced a smile. My skin and hair might have been flawless, but my tired eyes weren't just weary from Gable's secrets—they held some of my own.

My phone dinged with a text notification.

It was from Brave. For the first time, I wasn't riddled with annoyance at seeing his name on my screen.

Brave: *Hey sis. I just wanted to check in on you to see how you're doing.*

Me: *I'm doing OK.*

Brave: *Good. Have you heard from Gable or any word on how he's doing?*

Me: *No. I am actually heading to see him in a few.*

Brave: *OK. If you don't mind, can you keep me posted?*

Me: *I'll do my best.*

Brave: *That's all you can do.*

Me: *Thanks.*

Me: *I spoke to Justin, the attorney at my firm, today. He's open to chatting with you about your options. Can you meet him tomorrow? At my office. At noon. I won't be there, but you can meet him without me. We don't want to drag this out too long.*

Brave: *Sure thing. Tomorrow it is.*

Brave: *I love you, sis.*

I stared at Brave's last message. He'd always been affectionate, always telling me he loved me, but I'd never said it back.

Re-reading his words, a wave of sadness laced with guilt washed over me.

I hovered, unsure how to respond when a notification from my doorbell camera app alerted me that someone was approaching the door. I didn't have to look to know it was Neveah and Aurora.

I grabbed my mini backpack purse and headed toward the front door.

I didn't want Neveah and Aurora to come inside. If they did, they'd get cozy, and we would be here longer than I wanted.

I was ready to get this visit with Gable done and over with so I could breathe just a little better than I had since the day Gabriella told me that he wanted to see me.

I hadn't even made it out of the door yet, and already, the nausea was making waves in my gut.

The hour-long ride to the treatment facility was charged with conversations, laughs, and car karaoke. I was glad I decided to bring my girls along. Their company made the ride not just bearable but entertaining—far better than the lonely silence I would have endured on my own.

But as Neveah pulled into the parking lot of the facility, the anxiety that had lost most of its edge during the car ride began to recharge, humming low in the pit of my stomach.

After Neveah shifted her car into park, Aurora reached forward from the back seat and placed a gentle hand on my shoulder.

"Can we pray before you go in, sis?" she asked.

I nodded. "Of course." My stomach churned nervously. "I've got a strong feeling I am going to need all the prayers I can get."

Joining hands, we bowed our heads as Aurora led the prayer.

As Aurora prayed for peace in the midst of all the turbulence that had jolted me from my comfort zone, a sliver of hope washed over me.

Hope that this visit wouldn't break me down any more than the strain of the situation already had.

After our Amens, they pulled me into a group embrace. The warmth and love that radiated from within my sister circle was something that I'd always been deeply grateful for. These hugs had gotten the three of us through some rough patches—from middle and high school drama to college heartbreaks.

We had our share of disagreements, but this moment was just more proof that the bond between us was still as strong as ever.

We separated from our circle of comfort, and exchanged our habitual, *I love yous.*

I turned toward the massive facility, took a long inhale, exhaled slowly, and walked toward the unknown.

Inside, I took the elevator up to the third floor as instructed by the woman at the information desk.

The ride was short, but each moment was stretched thin with anticipation.

When the elevator doors slid open, I stepped into a smaller, more intimate lobby, but no less intimidating. A second information desk sat ahead.

I approached the desk slowly, each step syncing with the rapid beat of my heart.

Breathe, Blou. I coached myself to stay calm.

"Hi. How may I help you?" the woman at the desk said with a smile.

I returned it with one that didn't quite reach my eyes. "I'm here to see Gable Whitmore."

"One second." She clicked through a few screens.

"May I have your name please?" she asked, her eyes still on the monitor.

"Blou Rivers-Whitmore."

"Ah." She smiled. "Mrs. Rivers-Whitmore, please sign in on the clipboard in front of you and have a seat, please."

I scribbled my name and the time on the sign-in sheet, my hands trembling slightly, making the letters uneven.

I turned to a chair in the far corner of the lobby, hoping for a moment to collect myself. But before I could sit down, the brown door beside the desk swung open.

"Mrs. Rivers-Whitmore?" A young lady who looked to be in her mid-to-late twenties held the door open.

"Yes." I answered, even though I was the only person in the waiting area.

"Hi. I'm Tesha, Mr. Whitmore's nurse. Right this way, please."

I followed her through the door and halfway down a long, quiet hallway.

"I hope it's not a problem," she said glancing back at me, "but we require all visitors to wear a mask over their nose and mouth at all times, scrubs over your clothing, a hair covers, and shoe covers."

I nodded. "OK," I said.

She led me into a room with lockers and a small sink. The lockers reminded me of the small room I peeked into from a quaint waiting area when I accompanied Aunt Gina once to a mammogram appointment.

"Here is everything you need." She handed me the stack of items she'd mentioned. "You can leave your purse and phone inside one of the lockers and create a four-digit code to retrieve your belongings after the visit. Please wash your hands at the sink before you come out."

I nodded again. This process alone was going to overwhelm me before I even laid eyes on my husband.

Left alone, I slid everything on and placed my bag and phone into the locker.

Before locking it, I pulled my phone back out and texted our group chat.

Me: *I'm a little creeped out, y'all.*

Neveah: *Why?*

Me: *Because I have to cover my entire body before entering his room.*

Aurora: *OK?*

Me: *It's making me think the worst.*

Neveah: *Maybe it's just procedural. He is very sick, right?*

Me: *OK. I have to leave my phone in a locker so if you message me I can't respond until I am done.*

Aurora: *You got this. *Prayer hands* *Heart emoji**

I placed my phone back into the locker, closed it and entered Gable's birth month and day—*0423*.

After washing my hands, I opened the door. The nurse stood outside waiting for me.

"Ready?" she asked with a smile.

I shrugged. "Just as ready as I'm going to be."

She gave me an understanding smile, the kind I'm sure she'd given many times to both the patients and their loved ones.

"Tesha, right?" I asked when we stopped in front of Room 619.

She turned to look at me. "Yes, ma'am."

Shaking my head, my brows furrowed. "You can call me

Blou," I said softly. "What can I expect when I go in there?"

She sighed. "I'm really not supposed to talk to the visitors about the status of the patients."

I nodded. My gaze slid to the closed door.

"But," she said, resting a gentle hand on my arm. I met her empathic eyes.

"Mr. Whitmore has told me so much about you." The corners of her mouth curled into a tender smile. "I will just say, he's been making some small strides over the past few days."

Blinking back the tears welling in my eyes, I swallowed the lump that had formed in my throat. I couldn't go into Gable's room a crying mess.

"Are you ready to go in?" Tesha asked softly, placing her hand on the doorknob.

I nodded.

She twisted the knob, opening Gable's world to me—the world I knew nothing about, yet it had drastically altered the course of my own.

I eased into the dimly lit room, bracing myself to find Gable weak and barely coherent. Instead, he sat propped up on pillows, reading.

It wasn't like a typical hospital room. His bed had an oak head-board, like one you'd find in a home bedroom, paired with an adjustable mattress. A matching dresser and a two-drawer nightstand matched the headboard, completing the set. A recliner sat beside a wide window, and a writer's desk was in the corner.

Despite its homey touches, it wasn't enough to disguise the somber feel of the medical facility. The dismal ambience of borrowed time lingered in the atmosphere. The IV and rhythmically beeping monitor displaying his vitals were a reminder of exactly where I was. The slow, steady beep of the machine was no competition for my racing heartbeat.

He looked up from the book he held. His caramel complexion was as smooth as it had been that last morning when he'd kissed me so deeply it felt like a long goodbye. Unbeknownst to me, he was fully aware he was about to upend the quiet life we'd built.

He looked up at me, and a smile spread across his handsome face. His thinner frame made the weight he had lost during the treatment unmistakable, but he was no less beautiful than he'd been before—the same low haircut, the same neatly trimmed beard.

"You came." His tired eyes sparked to life, flickering with something that looked like gratitude.

"Yeap." I stepped past Tesha, farther into the room. "I did."

"Mr. Whitmore," Tesha said. Both Gable and I turned toward her. "If you need anything you know how to reach me. Remember the safety rules: Your visitors must keep their mask on. Can't have you getting sick with your compromised immune system."

She smiled in my direction. "I'll leave you two alone."

Her mask was pulled under her chin. I assumed she didn't put it on because she hadn't come far into the room.

"Thank you, Tesha," Gable said politely. His eyes followed her to the door, before settling back on me.

"Come, sit." He patted the space beside him on the full-size bed.

Instead, I sank into the recliner.

"I haven't seen you in all this time, and no hug? Kiss?" He smirked.

The image of the little boy in the photos flickered through my mind. His deep dimples lighting up his chubby cheeks when he smiled, identical to the ones that now dented Gable's coy grin.

I shot him a heated glare.

Barely five minutes in, and he was already starting to get under my skin.

With the heaviness of his secret hanging over me, the thought of touching him made my stomach turn.

I had no idea what I would feel when I saw him. I didn't know if I would want to hold him or slap him. The latter was winning.

I ignored his advances and the fire rising inside of me. Steadying my breathing, I scanned his face. "You look well," I said, my voice taut but composed.

He sighed. "Looking well and being well are two different

things."

His eyes didn't waver. "It's been a rollercoaster. Fortunately, you caught me on one of my better days."

"What is this illness called and what are the doctors saying about your prognosis?" I asked, the tension melting off my stiff shoulders.

He turned his gaze to the muted television, credits rolling across a Seinfeld re-run. Silence thickened the air between us.

He straightened and swung his legs over the side of the bed but remained seated. Instead of a hospital gown, he wore plaid pajama pants and a short-sleeve t-shirt.

Our eyes met. Something unspoken passed through the space between us.

"It's called, viscerimatosis. It affects the blood, then attacks the organs. They gave me all my doses," he said quietly, "then transferred me here—home." His voice cracked. "If my labs stay steady over the next couple of weeks, I'll be released from the program. I'll take meds for the rest of my life. I could live a very close-to-normal life with the meds." His lips curled into a warm smile, but his eyes remained vacant and unmatched.

I leaned in slightly. "And if they aren't?" I asked, gently.

He swallowed hard. For a moment, I thought he would look away, but he didn't.

"There will be nothing else they can do for me." His voice was almost a whisper. "They will refer me to a specialist—someone familiar with this type of illness—but I would pretty much be on my own until the end, which wouldn't be far off—wouldn't be long before my organs start to completely shut down."

I gasped. The news hit like a rushing wind, knocking the breath from my lungs.

"Gable, I—" I didn't resist the tears pressing behind my eyes, threatening to break. I rose from the recliner and moved toward him.

"I'm really sorry this is happening to you." I wrapped my arms around his neck and sobbed into the frail curve of his shoulder.

He placed a hand gently on my waist and drew back just

enough to meet my eyes.

"Shhh. Don't you cry for me, my love," he said, voice hushed and trembling.

The tears he'd been forcing back began to slide down his cheeks.

I closed my eyes and rested my forehead gently against his. Emotion surged between us.

He lifted his eyes to meet mine. "This is what I was trying to protect you from, Blou." He planted a soft kiss on my cheek. "I hate to see you hurting."

The reminder of what he'd kept from me sent a ripple of anger through my body. I recoiled.

"So keeping this from me was more about you protecting yourself?" I crossed my arms, my gaze hard and unflinching.

His brows creased. He tilted his head. "What?"

"You said you hate to see me hurting."

"I do," he snapped, irritation rising. "What is wrong with you?"

"What is wrong with me?" I barked. "You made a life-changing decision for me without even consulting me, and you're asking me that question? You know what I think? I think you saw the pain your mother went through when your father left her, and it's a trigger for you to see me in pain because it reminds you of her pain."

"That's insane. I'm not even going to respond to that." He looked away.

"But that's just it, Gable. I couldn't see it before, but I can clearly see it now. Every time grief gets heavy for me on my mom's or dad's birthday, on holidays when I'm missing them the most, whenever I am deeply emotional, you always find something else to do, except to be around me. You hate your father for what he did, but you turned around and left me too."

He shook his head, releasing a sardonic chuckle.

"This is different," he said.

"Barely," I retorted.

"Don't you ever compare me to him." His voice hardened.

"I'm the one who's sick, Blou. "Are you really this selfish? Are you really going to make this about you and your…your fixation on your parents' death? You aren't always the victim."

I narrowed my eyes at the audacity.

"I think it's time for me to go," I said, my voice cracking under the weight of his words.

The tension slipped from his face. "Blou." He reached for me.

I stepped back again.

"I'm sorry." He shook his head, slow and weary. "This is just a lot. I can admit I have some issues with seeing you hurting. Who wants to see the person they love hurting? Please believe me when I tell you I was really thinking of protecting you."

"Why did you think leaving me in the dark would protect me?" My voice softened, but the ache remained.

"I didn't know if I would live or die." His jaw flexed. "Hell, I still don't know. I knew you would be upset if I left, but I thought leaving would be easier for you than watching me go through—" He threw his hands up and looked around. "All of this." His shoulders sank in defeat. "But maybe I didn't handle it in the best way." He shook his head. "This condition is…I didn't want you to have to take care of me too."

"Then why call me here now?"

He looked away, his gaze downcast. "After Gabriella told me you found those letters, I—" He paused, his eyes finding mine again. "I knew I had to see you. If I had any chance of keeping you."

I scowled. "You've kept a baby from me our entire marriage, and you think you can keep me?"

He shrugged. "Look, I'm sorry for that."

He reached for me again. I took another small step back.

"But the baby was conceived before you and I married. I cared about her and how she felt."

"Your baby was born the same year we married."

As if I hadn't spoken, he continued, "She had been a good friend of mine for a long time. The arrangement I had with his mother was between me and her." He released a deep breath.

"And I just didn't see how that had anything to do with you…us. We agreed I would not be an active part of the baby's life, and I haven't—just pictures from time to time."

My eyes widened. Both rage and amusement mingled in my chest. I laughed in disbelief. I couldn't believe what I was hearing. This did not sound like the Gable I knew. But maybe Aurora was right. Maybe this was who he had been all this time, and I was just too blind to see it: a jackass.

He stared at me. "What's so funny?" he asked, his nostrils flaring.

"You didn't want to give me children." His tone was laced with resentment. "Even though you could have."

I stopped laughing. My glare cut through him.

This conversation kept getting more unbelievable by the second.

He let out a brittle laugh. "You really are something else, you know that?" Shaking his head, his piercing gaze stuck to me, un-movable. "You aren't without your own secrets, Blou."

I crossed my arms. "And just what is that supposed to mean?"

Looking away, he let out a venomous chuckle before focusing back on me.

"You really think I don't know, don't you?"

Narrowing my eyes, I deepened my glare. "I already know Ga-briella told you that she saw Zamir and me out, but—"

"Just stop." His voice raised slightly; his jaw clenched tighter. "I know about the baby."

I froze. "Baby?" I repeated. My voice shook.

His watery eyes flashed with something raw and painful. "I know, Blou. I know what you did," he said just above a whisper, defeat pressed against his sagging shoulders.

Tears welled in my eyes as an overwhelming rush of guilt flooded my heart when the realization shook me. I knew exactly what he was talking about. But how? Suddenly, the tables turned on me, and I was reeling. Light-headedness swayed my balance, but I remained on my feet.

"Gable…I-I'm sorry," I uttered softly, cautiously.

"I'm sorry you aborted my baby too," his comeback was quieter than I expected his next words to be. His wet eyes, fatigued by the pain of the secret I'd carried throughout our entire relationship. A single tear slipped down his cheek.

He continued, not moving his eyes from me. "I saw the papers in your nightstand drawer one morning after I stayed the night with you." He looked toward the floor, wiping tears from his face. "I was looking for a pen to leave you a note so I didn't have to wake you, and I saw them." Swallowing hard, he sucked in a long deep breath. "I decided not to say anything—see if you would tell me. When you never bought it up, I figured we were even, and I would let you keep your little secret to yourself."

Closing my eyes, I quietly inhaled and released a steady breath. Memories of the day I went to the clinic flashed behind my eyelids. Aurora driving me there. Neveah staying the night with me, comforting me as I cried myself to sleep—not in agreement but also not judging. I avoided Gable for two days, pretending I was swamped with cases from work and needed to focus all my time on preparations for court.

"Gable," I said softly.

Casting his eyes back on mine, he too released an exhale, blinking back more tears.

"It wasn't your baby."

His brows knitted together. "What?"

"It was Zamir's baby," I said in a hushed tone, my voice faltering. "I was pregnant when I met you. I just didn't know yet. I was eight weeks when I found out."

A silent understanding filled the small space between us. He released a heavy sigh of relief. His tired eyes softened into tender thoughtfulness.

"Wow." Feeling sympathetic, I took a step toward him, wanting to comfort him but I thought better of it and kept my distance.

"All this time, you thought I had gotten pregnant by you, aborted your baby, kept it from you and then married you?"

He opened his mouth to speak but nothing came. Clearing his throat to make way for his words, he leaned in slightly. "Would you have had it…I mean…if y'all were still together at the time?"

It was my turn to look away. I shook my head. "I don't know, honestly."

He scoffed. "But without a doubt you know you wouldn't have mine. You refused to even think about it when I asked."

"Gable, you knew before we got married that I didn't want kids, but you still wanted to marry me. You rushed to marry me."

I let the truth land between us, shooting him an exasperated look.

"Was it because Zamir showed up at Aunt Gina's and you thought I'd go back to him?"

His gaze dropped to the floor. A quiet clarity filled the space we had once cherished as a deep love. In the background of our chaos, the steady chirp of the machine never wavered unlike the faltering hope of our marriage.

"Yeah," I said, quietly. "I know about Zamir coming by. You told him you were my husband."

Gable lifted his eyes to mine. Surrendering to the drastic turn in our relationship, he paused, careful of his next words.

"Blou, you're right," he said softly. "I agreed to no children, but I thought you would eventually change your mind. That's on me. I truly am sorry." His voice cracked with sincerity. "Please, all I ask is for a little grace."

I knew Gable well enough to know when he was truly sorry. But where his regrets fell were lost on me. I wasn't quite sure which deceit he was apologizing for.

A wave of nausea curled low in the pit of my stomach as a funereal epiphany darkened the room. The burden of the truth pressed heavily against my chest, shortening my breathing just under the mask I wore.

His regret was our marriage. He knew he never should have marriage me. I knew it too.

He reached for me. Again.

And this time, I stepped toward him, entering his space and allowing him to wrap his arms around me in a warm embrace.

My arms hung at my sides, awkward and unready, as my mind

caught up with the sensation of being engulfed in his familiarity. Although my mind fought to resist how my body responded to his touch, for a moment, the ache inside me quieted.

Empathy crept in, ripping away at the anger that consumed me just moments ago. I melted into him like warm butter, letting the tension roll off my shoulders.

"Blou," he said, just above a whisper, gently releasing me, "I feel lightheaded. I need to lie down."

His words jolted me from the brief calmness I had sank into. "Are you OK?" My eyes searched his, scanning for something—anything—favorable that could calm the panic rising inside of me.

"Should I call Tesha? Where is your call button?" I helped him ease back on the bed, slow and careful.

He closed his eyes, breath shallow, waiting for it to steady before he spoke. "I'm OK," he said, though his breathing was labored. "Sometimes I get a little short of breath and light-headed."

I gently rested my hand on his shoulder. Noticing a cup of water on the nightstand, I asked, "Do you need your water?"

Before he could answer, the door creaked open, and Tesha strolled in with a wide grin that quickly faded as she stepped closer.

"Mr. Whitmore." She paused, her brows knitting together. She eyed the numbers glowing on the monitor, the beeping suddenly louder in the quiet room. "I came to tell you that you have another visitor waiting, but…" She glanced at me, then pulled a small note pad and pen from her shirt pocket, scribbling something down quickly. "Your pressure is up too high. I'm sorry Mrs. Rivers-Whitmore," she said gently, tenderness in her eyes, "when this happens, we have to cut visitation short so he can rest, undisturbed." She looked at Gable apologetically. "I'll inform your other visitor."

I nodded, my gaze shifting back to Gable.

"Tesha, please let her…my visitor…that I'd like her to call me. She knows how to reach me."

She nodded. "Will do."

He reached for my hand, slow and deliberate, gently closing

his fingers around mine. His lips curled into a faint smile.

"I'll see you later?" he asked. His eyes searched mine, quietly pleading for something reassuring to hold on to.

"I nodded, hesitant, not quite sure when, or under what circumstances, I would see him next.

Tesha placed a gentle hand on my shoulder.

"I'll walk you back to the locker room."

I gave Gable's hand a light squeeze before following Tesha out of the room, dragging with me the heaviness of every truth I had stumbled upon during this visit.

After stripping off the cover-ups and gathering my things, Tesha walked me back to the lobby door. When I pushed open the doors of the waiting area, I expected to see Gabriella. Tesha had said Gable had another visitor. I couldn't think of anyone else who would come to see him other than his sister, or who knew how to contact him.

Did anyone else know he was here? I wondered quietly.

I glanced around. No one was there.

"Mrs. Rivers-Whitmore, can you please sign out, please?"

I turned toward the desk. The receptionist stood behind it, holding the clipboard out to me.

"Sure." I took the pen from a cup labeled *Clean*, then accepted the clipboard from her hand. I glanced at the clock on the wall and penned the time into the check-out space, just beside where I'd written my name earlier.

Just as I was about to place the clipboard down, a familiar name caught my eye—a familiar handwriting.

My heart leaped with confusion.

Esa Collins.

I blinked at the name on the sheet, noticing how the curves of this signature were almost identical to the one on Esa and Zamir's divorce decree. I gasped. It had suddenly dawned on me how similar her signature was to the one signed, *Your Old Pal*, on the letters in Gable's safe.

"Is everything OK?" the receptionist asked.

I pulled my gaze from the paper and looked up.

"Um. Yes."

I handed it to her.

"Thank you," I said, just barely above a whisper.

I moved toward the elevator, each footstep heavier than the last, dragging today's baggage with me like a ball on a chain around my ankle.

As the elevator slid open, the door to the family restroom swung wide. A little boy burst into the lobby, giggling.

"Amir. Walk, please," a familiar voice called behind him, following from the bathroom.

I quickly slipped into the elevator, rapidly pressing the close button repeatedly, willing it to shut before Esa saw me. My gaze met the eyes of the familiar little boy with the chubby cheeks and deep dimples right before the door closed shut completely. I jabbed the button for the first floor and collapsed against the cold steel wall.

My stomach twisted into knots, breath quick and shallow. Hands trembling as if I had seen a ghost.

My thoughts raced, darting from one scenario to the next. I didn't know what to make of what I had just seen.

Esa Collins.

And the little boy in the pictures from Gable's safe. Amir.

Chapter *twenty-one*

All night, I had tossed and turned, ruminating about the many ways I felt betrayed.

Why were Esa and Amir at Gable's facility? Could it be a co-incidence—were they there to see another patient?

Could I be mistaken and the child in the photos merely resembled Amir?

No. They had to be there to see Gable.

Amir was the child in the photos.

He was Gable's child.

No matter how much I wanted to deny what I knew to be true, I couldn't.

Had Zamir known all along and kept this from me?

My stomach soured, bitterness rising in my throat. I jumped out of bed, rushed into the bathroom and lunged toward the toilet, spilling this morning's coffee into the bowl.

Yes, I had kept a pregnancy and abortion from the two of them but that was different. Gable and I had only been dating for a month and a half, and Zamir and I were over. I didn't think we would ever talk again. He had his life and career miles away, and I didn't want a baby anyway. I couldn't have a baby and risk my greatest fear happening, so I did what I had to and kept it between me and my two best friends.

From the other room, my phone rang.

I had ignored every call since Neveah and Aurora dropped me off at home last night. Neveah had offered to stay over for moral support after I spilled the tea on the way home about my visit with Gable. I insisted on being alone and politely declined her offer.

I splashed water on my face, rinsed my mouth, stumbled back to my bed and buried myself under the covers.

My phone rang again.

Without moving the covers from over my head, I reached toward my nightstand, felt for the phone, and pulled it under the covers. The glow from the display screen illuminated my dark mood. I browsed through missed calls. Brave had called four times. A spark of concern flickered in my gut.

I tapped the call button, placed the phone on speaker, and laid it beside me.

"Hey, sis," he said, his tone dancing with excitement.

"Hey, Brave," I murmured.

He hesitated. "You OK?"

"Yeah," I lied. "Just tired." I added, lifted my voice slightly, giving it a gentle rise to mask the murkiness beneath.

"Oh. OK," he said, uncertainty in his voice but willing to follow my lead. "I got some good news."

"Oh?" I said, my interest slightly piqued. "What's up?"

"Justin said I can use video footage to prove Tyrek misled me and that his behavior was unethical."

"How so? "I wasn't aware of any video footage."

"Yeah. I have a video recording with sound inside and outside of my house and a camera doorbell. Smart, huh?"

I chuckled. "Yeah."

"I also have the email I sent him with the original contract attached. I stated it was the last and final version. I listed the vendors and everyone who was named in the contract for other purposes and I asked Tyrek to reply with confirmation that no one was left out."

"And?" I sat up freeing myself from the dark abyss of my covers and propping up on my pillows.

"And," he continued, "he replied to the email, confirming the list was correct. His name wasn't listed."

"But couldn't he argue that you later discussed changes that were not in the email?"

"He could. That's the same thing I asked Justin."

"What did he say?"

"On one of the videos, Tyrek raved about how sweet of a deal I was getting and how he wished he could be a part of my business. I told him this was something I wanted to do on my own. I didn't need any partners. Justin said with that video and the emails that should be enough to build a case against Tyrek."

"But that's not the only video," he added. "I happened to be going back through my doorbell camera vids. Don't ask me why I do that. I just do, periodically, and I'm glad I did."

"What did you find?"

"The day before I signed the contract, Tyrek came by. He stepped outside to take a call. He told him to add his name to the contract as a silent partner. My doorbell camera picked up everything."

"And you're sure he was talking to the attorney?"

"Had to be. He told the attorney not to worry about something—said he had a way to get me to sign it. I don't know what the attorney said, but then Tyrek said, 'Yes, tomorrow at your office.'"

"*Mmm.* Interesting," I said, getting out of bed and heading to the kitchen to make coffee.

"Yeah," he agreed. "After I let him in, he said he came by to talk to me about the vendors—said he spent a lot of time getting me connected to them and didn't want to risk losing them. He told me they were going to go with someone else if I didn't lock in the deals by the end of the next day and that he had an attorney who could look everything over for me. "And the next day, who did we meet with?" he asked rhetorically. "None other than, the attorney," he said answering his own question.

"Wow. That's crazy." I was genuinely intrigued. I was still annoyed he got into this mess, but aside from me hooking him up with Justin, he seemed to be doing everything he could to fix it on his own.

"OK. So, what's Justin going to do next?" I asked. I placed a mug on the single-serve coffee maker and pressed the brew button.

"Nothing."

I frowned. "What do you mean nothing?"

"You sure you're ready for this next part?" His voice danced with playfulness, and I could practically see the wide grin on his face.

I rolled my eyes but couldn't help giggling at his giddiness. "Boy, get on with it."

"OK. OK." He laughed. "I went to see Tyrek."

My eyes widened. "You did *what*? Why would you—"

He cut in. "Wait. Before you get your panties in a bunch, let me explain."

"Well, hurry up and tell me something because the last time you went to see him, you ended up in the hospital."

"Ouch, big sis," he teased. "You spare no feelings."

I placed my hand on a hip. My tolerance was shifting quickly to a lot less than it was at the beginning of this call.

"Brave," I said, scowling, "stop beating around the bush and start talking. Why did you go see him?"

"To negotiate, but…" he added quickly, "I didn't go alone."

I released a deep sigh. I took my coffee into the gathering room and settled on the couch.

"Do tell." I rolled my eyes, my impatience growing.

Getting a full story in a short time frame from this kid reminded me of what it used to be like when using dial-up internet—slow to connect and slower to load.

"Now, don't be mad when I tell you this."

"Who…went…with…you?" My patience was hanging on by a thread.

"Za-mir," he said slowly as if that would lessen the blow.

I froze. Silence stretched between us, filled with a flood of questions. I waited for him to continue.

"He called me a few weeks ago—said you'd shared some of the details about what happened to me. He was just calling to encourage me and pray with me if I was open to it. Since then, we've been talking. I kept him posted on everything. When I told him that I was planning to talk to Tyrek in person, he offered to go with me—said I shouldn't go alone, and he was happy to help in any way that he could."

My face flushed with warmth as anger spread through my body like wildfire. I couldn't believe Zamir. Yes, he'd been like a big brother to Brave before we broke up, but where did he get off inserting himself into my family's affairs without asking me?

I didn't know if I was so heated now because I was already angry with him. He had to know Gable was Amir's father, and he'd kept it from me.

Now this.

Could I trust anyone?

As soon as I hung up with Brave—If I ever hung up with Brave at the rate he was giving me information—I was going to call Zamir and rip him a new one.

"Blou? You there?"

"Um. Yeah," I said, my tone steady but slightly tensed.

"I asked Tyrek to meet me at London's, you know that café over in Cam Ridge Plaza?" he went on, not giving me a room to answer. "At first, he was skeptical, like he didn't want to meet me, but I reminded him how we've been friends since our freshman year in high school, and we shouldn't let our friendship go down the drain over this."

I frowned. "I know darn well, you don't still want to be his friend, Brave."

"No. Just listen, please," he said, firm but calm. "Anyway. He agreed to meet me. Zamir caught a video of us sitting together and then slid in the booth behind us without Tyrek noticing. First, I asked if he was willing to be bought out of the contract—not that I planned to do that, but it was a part of the plan. Can you believe he wanted triple what it cost me to start up? Anyway, I told him how ridiculous that was and how he was never supposed to be in the contract in the first place. His reply was all I needed." He paused.

"What was his reply?" I asked, sitting up straight, anxious to know what was coming next.

"He said that a real friend would have let him get in on the deal without him having to take matters into his own hands, that I was making a big deal out of nothing. That we can grow this business into something huge and then I would thank him for adding his name as a silent partner."

"Whoa," I said, amused, "and Zamir got all this recorded?"

"Yes." His tone was laced with satisfaction.

"But that video wouldn't be admissible in court. You didn't tell him you were recording."

"I never planned to use the video in court. Zamir sent me the video.

I pulled it up and showed it to Tyrek. I told him if he didn't sign an amendment to the contract releasing himself, I would show this video to the vendors and post it online. Those vendors will never do any type of business with him again. His reputation would tank—personally and professionally."

"Yikes," I said. "Did he sign it?"

"I already had the paperwork ready. I slid it across the table, and yes, he signed it."

"Woo. This is a lot." I sighed. "But at least it's over."

"Yep. Justin helped me make the proper corrections to my original contract, and I sent them over to the vendors via DocuSign."

"Wow, Brave." I collapsed back onto the couch. "I'm actually impressed."

"I was hoping—no, praying—you would be."

I could hear the relief in his voice.

"I've been waiting my whole life to hear you say that."

That comment gave me pause. I let his words sink in for a beat. Everything around me buzzed quietly as I pondered how to respond. I nodded, even though he couldn't see me. Taking a deep breath in, I let my shoulders sink on the exhale.

"Brave, I—"

"Blou," he interrupted, "we don't have to do this. Trust me, I'm good."

"I don't know that you are though." I tilted my head. "I don't know that I am either."

"What do you mean?" he asked.

"I've been horrible to you—blaming you for a tragedy that wasn't your fault, treating you like how you feel doesn't matter—like you didn't also lose my…our…mother too."

I took another deep breath and released it. "You didn't deserve that. I should have shown you love instead of bitterness. I've been a really bad sister. I'm sorry."

Silence lingered on the other end of the phone.

"Thank you for saying that." His voice cracked.

"Wait. Are you crying?" I asked.

He chuckled. "Well, it's not every day that a bad sister apologizes. Your therapist must be the best in the country," he teased.

I laughed. "I guess I deserve that."

"But really, Blou. You've helped me too, regardless of how hard it's been for you. Your grief. Everything you're going through now. You've still found it in your heart to help me."

I could hear him inhale and blow it out.

"That's not just love, sis. That's grace, and for that, I love you."

I smiled. Warmth spread slowly in my chest, melting away the iciness that had resonated there years ago. A gentle sense of freedom washed over me, making room for something sweet and tender—a place just for my baby brother. "I love you too."

Chapter *twenty two*

"Girl, I'm so glad you got that situation off of your plate," Neveah said. Sitting in her office chair, she swiveled from side to side. The window in her office spanned the entire wall.

"Yeah. Me too," I said, "but Tyrek would have never had the opportunity to inveigle his way into the contract if Brave had listened to me in the beginning."

She squinted into the camera, her expression a sharp reminder. "I thought you were—"

Cutting her off, I raised my hands. "I know, I know. I said I was putting it behind us. I was just going to say, that it's in the past now, and we're moving forward."

"In other news, can we please get the spa date on the calendar?" Neveah asked.

"OK. I'm going to schedule it. We need it. I feel like we've barely had a chance to catch up since I went to see Gable."

"I know, girl. I've been super busy with work stuff."

"I'm back y'all," Aurora jumped into view. "That was Layla's sitter at the door. She came by to get the money we owed her for picking up Layla from school and watching her when we took you to see Gable."

My and Neveah's faces scrunched in confusion.

"You're just now paying her?" I asked.

"Right. That was like, a few weeks ago," Neveah added.

Aurora shrugged. "I tried several times to either take it to her or have her come pick it up, but she said she was busy between her classes and her internship. We had to find a backup sitter because she's been so busy."

"Why didn't you just Cash App it to?" Neveah asked.

I waited for the answer to the same question I was going to ask.

"For a young adult, she's weird about things like that," Aurora said. "She said she doesn't use digital payment services. She doesn't want to attach her card."

Neveah frowned. "Girl, what? She could use the Cash App card."

Aurora giggled. "Hey, I know, but it's not my business to pry." She shrugged. "I just pay her cash like she requested."

"That sounds fishy but OK." I pursed my lips.

"And how long have you known her?" Neveah asked.

"She's been babysitting Lay Lay for about six months. One of the moms in Layla's dance class referred me to her." Her gaze shifted between Neveah and me. She chuckled at our concerned faces. "She's good though. Y'all are overthinking."

"If you say so," I said.

"But in other news, Blou," Aurora said, quickly pivoting the conversation to me. "Speaking of Gable, what's up with him?"

I shrugged. "I haven't heard anything from Gable since our visit."

Both Neveah and Aurora's eyebrows furrowed.

"Why?" Neveah asked.

"I don't know." I fidgeted my coils, wrapping a few strains of curly hair around my finger. A tinge of guilt fluttered in my belly. "I haven't been back to see him. He hasn't called either. Neither did he offer me the phone number to his room."

"In other words, you're avoiding him since you saw that lady there. *Um*…what's her name?" She snapped her fingers, trying to recall Zamir's ex-wife's name.

I glared at her. "Esa," I said. "And yes, I guess you can say that. I mean, he said it would be a few weeks before he knew if the treatment worked for him. Either way, he'll be out soon, and I don't know how I'm going to approach this…us."

"Ugh. That's tough, boo," Neveah said. Her gaze held empathy.

"Yeah. It sucks but hey, nothing I can do but pray about it and try to make the best decision for me," I said. A dull ache nagged at my temple.

Aurora nodded. "Yes. True." She smiled, wistfully. "You talked to Zamir?"

I cleared my throat. "Nope. Been avoiding him too," I said quietly.

"Are you going to tell him about…you know, y'all's baby?" Neveah asked.

"Yeah, eventually." I shook my head. "I hate to even tell him with everything he's already going through. His divorce. His son being sick. But I will. Not sure when though. I was going to call him and give him a piece of my mind about helping Brave without telling me, but I decided against it."

Silence fell between us. The conversation had gotten heavier than I expected. I had a meeting in an hour. I needed to keep my head clear.

"Enough of that sad song." I giggled despite the tightness in my chest.

"Oh yeah, Veah. I almost forgot: How did your meeting go this morning?" I asked, shifting the attention to Neveah.

"Yeeeah. About that." A wide grin spread across her face. "This weekend…we're celebrating."

My eyes widened, mouth agape. "You made partner?" I squealed, leaning closer to the screen.

Neveah grabbed the phone from whatever she had propped it up on and stood. "Um. Not quite." Her eyes lit up.

My grin faded.

"Then what?" Aurora and I asked in unison, anticipating Neveah's next words.

"You ladies are looking at the owner of Wilkinson Consulting, Inc.," she sang.

My eyes grew even wider than before. "What?" I jumped from my chair. "You started your own firm?" I squealed again.

"Oh my goodness," Aurora said, just as shocked as I was.

Neveah nodded, her smile stretching wide.

"It's been in the works for a while, but I wanted to surprise y'all." She grinned. "In the meeting this morning, they did offer me partner, but I declined and put in my resignation."

"Congratulations." Aurora and I said synchronously. Both of us beamed, grinning from ear-to-ear.

"Let us know if there's anything we can do to help." I added.

"We are definitely celebrating this weekend," Aurora confirmed her eyes glowing with pride for our sister-friend.

The intercom button flashed on my desk phone, followed by a beep and Fallon's voice.

"Blou."

"Yes?"

"You have a visitor."

I frowned. "My meeting isn't for another fifty minutes."

"It's not your client. It's…" She hesitated. "It's Mr. Collins. Should I send him back?"

I looked into the screen at my friends, silently questioning them about what I should do. I wasn't sure if I was ready to talk to Zamir after he kept the truth from me about Gable being Amir's father. And even though what he did for Brave was a good thing, I still felt a little betrayed that he didn't tell me what was going on.

"Blou, are you there?" Fallon asked.

I pressed the talk button. "*Um*. Yeah" I replied. "One second."

"Girl, get your butt off this phone and go talk to that man," Aurora chimed in.

"I gotta go anyway," Neveah said. "I've only got a few weeks to tie up all the loose ends before I am done here—discuss my accounts with the partner and get them transferred over to someone else."

"I…" I hesitated. "OK. I'll talk to y'all later."

"OK," Aurora said, blowing a kiss at the screen. "I love y'all."

"Love you too, bookie," I said, blowing a kiss back.

"I love you too," Neveah said. "Talk later." She disconnected the call.

Then Aurora hung up.

I told Fallon she could send Zamir in. I pulled out the compact mirror I kept in my desk and quickly inspected my face and my teeth, making sure there was no spinach lodged in them from this morning's omelet. I lightly fluffed my fresh wash-and-go curls and placed the mirror back into my desk drawer right as Zamir walked in.

My jaw locked, and my eyes narrowed at the sight of him, but my stomach was not in agreement with whatever my face had going on. The visceral reaction to this man was still the same after all these years regardless of how mad I was at him. My gut betrayed my attitude with flutters, flips, and kicks. *The more I get used to being around him again, I'm sure these feelings will subside,* I thought, swallowing hard, forcing down the lump in my throat—if I even remained his friend after his dishonesty.

He strolled closer, looking as fine as ever in a white T-shirt fitted just enough to hug his firmly sculpted chest. His face, soft and gentle, was totally contrary to my stiff features.

I remained seated behind my desk. He took a seat in the chair across from me. Our eyes met—a torched flame still in mine; something else in his.

"What are you doing here?" I asked, my tone firm.

"I've been calling and texting you. You haven't responded." He tilted his head. "Everything OK?"

My gaze burned into him. Silence lingered in the thick air between us. The quiet hum of the mini fridge tucked in the corner of my office triggered a reminiscence of the day we broke up in his apartment.

A sadness washed over me, fueling my anger.

His brow furrowed. "Are you OK?" he asked, a warm gleam in his eyes.

Straightening my posture, I leaned in. "No, Zamir," I snapped. "Would you be OK if someone you thought was a friend lied to you or hid important details that greatly affect your life?"

Confusion riddled his face. "Blou, what are you talking about?" he asked, his voice calm and steady.

I rolled my eyes. "Are you really going to do this?" I scoffed.

"Do what? Can you just tell me what's going on?" His voice rose slightly.

I shot him a look that warned him to keep his voice down.

His eyes softened. "I'm sorry. I didn't mean to raise my voice," he said, leaning in. "Tell me what you're talking about."

Releasing my hard expression, I relaxed my shoulders but kept my gaze intensely on his. I was starting to think he really didn't know what I was talking about. If his character was anything like it was when we were younger, he was far from a liar.

I released a deep sigh.

"I saw Esa," I said, my voice cracking, "when I went to see Gable."

Zamir's brows drew together. He searched my face for clarity.

Reading his thoughts by his expression, I continued. "I was visiting Gable a few weeks ago." I cleared my throat. "When I was about to leave, I saw her name on the visitation log, then, before I got on the elevator, I saw her and Amir leaving the restroom."

His expression grew more obscure with each word I spoke. "What were they doing there?"

I shrugged. "Your guess is as good as mine."

"Wait…you already knew how Amir looked?"

"Well, Yeah." I nodded. "I didn't know who he was exactly until I saw him with Esa. I told you about Gable's illness and him leaving, but I never told you about the pictures."

"Pictures?" he questioned.

It was getting difficult to read what he was feeling as his body language and facial expressions shifted. It seemed like his emotions were all over the place, like he didn't know what to feel but was trying to display calmness.

"I found pictures of a child in Gable's office safe along with letters from the mother," I spoke gently. I had a feeling I was about to indulge him with new information that might wound him deeply. "There was one picture each year, starting when the child was a newborn."

His eyes glossed over with emotion, eyebrows drawn together as he anticipated my next words. I didn't know how much he knew or if he knew anything, but the blaze in his eyes told me all I needed to know.

He didn't know as much as I thought he did. I knew the fire behind his eyes that stood out the most among whatever else he was feeling was not for me.

"Are you OK," I asked.

He nodded. He blinked, holding back as much emotion as he could.

I felt an urge to reach out and touch him—comfort him. "Let's move to the couch."

After we silently settled in on the other side of the office, he stared at the wall straight ahead. *Dang. Has this man changed at all?* I thought as the memories of the day we broke up came back to mind again.

I placed an empathic hand over his. I had already had some time to process what I had found out, but this was all new to him.

He cleared his throat and swallowed hard. "So, from what you've told me…" he paused, turning to face me and locking his eyes on mine. "I gather, Amir is Gable's son?"

I nodded.

Closing his eyes, he took a deep breath and released it.

"I found out he wasn't mine months ago," he said in a hushed tone, a tear sliding down his cheek. "So, that's not new to me, but she wouldn't give me any information. She said I was his father and have always been, and that's all that mattered." He shook his head. "I pressed her for details, but she refused to give me any," he said through clinched teeth.

His shoulders sank. I wiped a tear from his cheek. His eyes fluttered open. He glanced at me before looking at my hand on top of his. He took my hand into his and gently squeezed, fixing his eyes back to the wall.

"How did you find out…that Amir isn't…" I hesitated.

"My child," he finished the sentence, snickering, the truth obviously hurtful but somewhat amusing.

"You know Amir is sick, right?"

I nodded, agreeing more than giving an answer.

"The first time he needed a transfusion, of course, I was more than ready to give my blood."

He settled deeper onto the couch. I followed his lead, sitting back and sliding closer until we were shoulder to shoulder, our hands pressed together, fingers interlocked, and eyes on the wall in front of us.

"That's when I found out Amir has O-positive blood type." He shook his head. "I'm A positive. I knew then he wasn't mine."

"*Um*. Yeah, because obviously both his parents would also have O-positive blood type," I said, softly.

He nodded. "Yeap. That's why I filed for divorce. She could have told me. Gave me the choice, you know." His voice strained under the pressure of his pain. "When I found out, I left. I refused to talk to her for a couple of weeks because at first, I couldn't stand the sight of her. But I knew Amir needed me—he needs me. I'm the only father he knows."

"Zamir, I am so sorry." I whispered. "For everything. I'm sorry this happened to you, and I'm sorry I jumped to conclusions thinking you—"

"Shh." Looking over at me, he gave my hand a gentle squeeze. "This happened to you too—in a way."

I rested my head on his shoulder and waited for his next words.

"She didn't tell me she was going to take him to see his…his biological…" His pain rode in on every word like a crashing wave flooding our souls. He hesitated. We let silence take possession of the room, momentarily settling the emotional high from the common aching we both felt.

"Does Gable…" he asked softly.

I straightened and looked over at him, confused.

He met my gaze. "Does Gable have O-positive blood type?"

I swallowed hard, shifting my gaze back to the wall and nodded. "He does."

He blinked back a fresh set of tears.

"You're a good man, Zamir" I said, barely above a whisper.

"Why do you say that?"

"Amir is not your child, and you're still choosing to be his dad."

"Yeah. Always will be," he said.

Minutes slipped by as we sat hand in hand. A calm quietness settled between us. Our soft breathing became the loudest sound in the room as we drifted deep in thought, letting our truths—both different and the same—mingle in the silence.

Suddenly, Zamir erupted with laughter.

I looked at him, puzzled.

"I'm sorry," he managed through the cackling.

The laughter must have been contagious because I started laughing just as hard. Tears streamed down my cheeks. Our eyes met as the giggling fits subsided.

"Isn't this so ironic?" he said.

"Right," I agreed. "Who would have thought we would be sitting together years after our breakup discussing the child our spouses had together, and we had no idea they even knew each other." I shook my head.

He rested his head back onto the couch. "Life is crazy."

"Super crazy."

The intercom from my desk phone sounded. "Mrs. Rivers-Whitmore, your client has arrived," Fallon's voice chirped.

I sighed deeply.

"Well, I guess that's my cue." Zamir said, rising from the couch.

I stood and faced him. "I guess so, friend," I said, smiling up at him.

He leaned down and pressed a kiss against my cheek. "Later, Blou Skies."

At the door, he turned back and winked before leaving me

standing, still smiling.

epilogue

I looked out the window of the beach house taking in the ocean, its beautiful mix of green and blue waves crashing into the shore as the wedding decorators and florists busied themselves mastering the art of what would soon be a beautiful wedding ceremony.

The rippling tides carried my thoughts away and back to the day Gable returned home two years ago, unexpected, unannounced, catching me completely off guard.

After the emotionally taxing conversation I had with Zamir earlier that day, as we processed the new revelation that changed both our lives forever, all I wanted to do was relax for the evening, unbothered.

I sat in the chaise working through day fifteen of a twenty-one-day spiritual and mental wellness devotional journal, *Grow On*, which Dr. Butler had recommended. When my phone dinged with a notification from the doorbell camera alerting me that motion had been detected, I hoped it was neither of my friends. The day had wreaked emotional havoc within me, and I just wanted to be alone.

Looking at the camera, I saw Gable outside the door rummaging through a bag, looking for his key, I assumed.

"What in the world?" I whispered to myself, stunned still, watching him search his belongings.

My heartbeat picked up, beating rapidly against the walls of my chest. I tossed the journal to the side and rushed to the front door.

With my hand on the knob, I took a long, deep breath, hesitating before pulling it open.

Gable looked up from his unsuccessful quest to find his house key.

Our eyes met.

"I was looking for my—" he started to explain, not taking his gaze from mine.

"Your key?" I asked softly. I stood in awe, blindsided. *He's really here*, I thought.

He dropped his bags, stepped toward me, and pulled me toward him, enclosing me in his embrace.

Taken by surprise, I slowly wrapped my arms around him, hugging him back. I buried my face into the curves of his chest, thankful to feel the warmth from his arms—though frail—around me once again. I was just happy that he was alive. I didn't know what was coming next, but at that moment, it was good to feel him.

Lulling me from my idle thoughts, strong arms wrapped around my waist from behind, bringing me back into the present. I smiled. My eyes still lingered on the ocean, but my mind was no longer on Gable.

"Hey, babe. In here hiding out, huh?" Zamir said, stooping just enough to kiss my cheek, then resting his chin on my shoulder.

I settled into his tender embrace. "Just enjoying the beautiful view."

"How are my babies?" he asked quietly, gently rubbing both his hands over my protruding belly.

I giggled. "I hope ready to come out." I placed my hands over his.

"Well, they have at least another two weeks to bake in that oven, my queen."

"What are you two lovebirds doing in here?" Aurora chirped from behind us. "Hiding from the wedding party?"

We turned to face her.

"Ouu. You look so pretty in that dress with your baby bump," she said, a silly grin wide across her face, "and you're glowing.

I rolled my eyes playfully. "Thank you, sis," I grinned back. "Where's Neveah?" I asked as Brave strolled in.

"Hello, hello, big sisters and big bro." His voice boomed as he joined us.

"Hey, big head," I said, stepping toward him. He eased his arms around me, pulling me into a gentle hug.

Pulling back, his eyes drifted to my baby bump. Bending down eye level to my stomach, he placed one hand on each side.

I jumped when I felt a swift flutter and then another.

Brave looked up at me, flashing a grin. "My niece and nephew are kicking because they know Uncle B is their favorite person already," he chuckled.

I giggled.

Aurora placed a hand on Brave's back. "Hold on, li'l bro," she said, smirking. "Just because you are a big time CEO with a booming cryptocurrency business now, you don't take the place of the godmother as their favorite."

He laughed. "Don't exaggerate, sis," he joked. "You're just one of the godmothers. Does Neveah know you're taking all the credit?"

Aurora laughed, giving him a playful pinch. "By the way, where did you get this Dirty White Tee, t-shirt?" she asked, smoothing it out where she'd pinched it.

"Online. As you know, lately I've been big on donating to cancer organizations, mainly because of my dad. I recently started donating to this company."

"Ah, OK. What's the name of the company?" she asked.

"This is the name." He tugged at his shirt. "The Dirty White Tee."

"Oh, cool. I'll check it out."

"Aren't y'all supposed to be helping the bride get ready for the wedding?" Aunt Gina fussed. She entered the room with Uncle Lance close behind her—both dressed in their Sunday's best.

"She asked for a little time alone, Aunt Gina," Aurora said, "but Blou and I were just heading back up there."

Looking at Zamir, she linked her arm through mine.

"I'm going to have to steal your wifey away for a while," she told him. "but I promise you'll survive without her."

She laughed at her own joke along with the rest of us.

"I'll try" Zamir jested. He pressed his soft lips against mine, letting them linger before pulling back. "Take care of my babies." He winked.

A wide grin spread across my face from ear to ear.

"Bye, Zamir," Aurora interrupted, gently pulling me with her toward the door.

We walked into the room we had spent the night in with Neveah after her bachelorette party. She sat at the vanity staring at her reflection.

"I can't believe I'm doing this," she said, tears welling in her eyes.

"Oh, goodness," Aurora said. "Girl, don't start because…"

"No." Neveah cut in. "I do want to do this. I just can't believe I'm doing this, finally."

I draped my arms over her shoulders. "Aw, sweetie," I coddled. "Yes, you are *finally* trusting yourself and your man. You deserve a happily-ever-after with someone who sees you and your worth." I smiled down at her.

Lifting from the vanity's chair, she looked between me and Aurora.

"I have about an hour and a half before I have to get dressed." An impish grin danced on her lips. "Let's go walk on the beach."

Aurora and I both frowned. "Are you sure?" she said. "You're not trying to be a runaway bride, are you?"

"And girl, I've already got my dress on."

She turned to Aurora. "Yes, I'm sure. I want to go for a stroll on the beach with my sisters one more time as a single woman," she said, then turned to me. "Here."

She picked up the blue flowy sundress I'd worn earlier from the bed. "Put this back on." She frowned. "Why are you dressed so early any…never mind. It doesn't even matter. Just change."

I giggled. "You act like you can't stroll the beach after you're married but OK. Whatever you want, bridezilla," I teased, turning around, signaling Aurora to zip down the back of my dress.

She rolled her eyes, helping me and Aurora slide the dress down. "You know what I mean," she said.

I sat on the bed and watched my friends as they pulled the dress from over my legs instead of over my neatly styled hair.

Some days, it didn't seem real that I was pregnant *and* carrying twins. Two years ago, no one could have told me this would be my future. Two years ago, I never thought Zamir and I would get married.

As we walked through the massive beach house Lukas had rented for his and Neveah's nuptials, the wedding planner and her staff zoomed around making last-minute touches, checking that everything was perfectly set.

We walked through the back doors, which were fully open to the paved porcelain lanai and pool deck and ran into Fallon.

"Hey, boss," she chirped, cheesing.

I narrowed my eyes. "It's Blou," I replied. "Girl, we are not at work."

She laughed. "Sorry." She leaned in to hug me. "Where's Brave?" she asked, glancing around.

"I don't know, but he's in there somewhere aggravating somebody." I smirked.

"OK. Thanks." She grinned, walking past us. "I'll find him."

We watched as she walked into the house.

"I still cannot believe those two are together," Aurora said.

"Me neither," I said, shaking my head. "No matter how hard I tried, I couldn't keep them apart."

Neveah laughed. "But he's been treating her good, right?" she asked, as we headed down the walkway to the beach.

I shrugged. "Far as I know. They both seem happy. I mind my business, but I told Brave if he hurt her and she quits on me, I'll break the leg Tyrek didn't."

"That's cold," Aurora said, laughing.

Neveah sighed loudly and stopped walking

Aurora and I stopped and looked at her, puzzled.

"Veah, you good?" I asked.

She smiled. "I'm better than good," she said. "Look at us. There's nothing that makes me happier than seeing all of us happy. Our entire circle is thriving. I got over my fear of baby mama drama and decided to marry the man who has treated me like a queen since day one and my business is thriving." She grabbed my hand. "And you, Blou, after everything you went through with Gable, you're married to your first love now. Despite your fear of having children, you'll be having two beautiful babies soon. Not to mention, you're partner at your firm now."

I smiled. "Yup. Everything worked out. For a minute, I thought Zamir would never speak to me again after I told him about the abortion."

"Yeah," Aurora said. "That was rough for him at first, but he's known your struggle since we were kids, so thankfully, he understood your decision."

"Right," I agreed. "I just can't believe my birth control failed me back then *and* again this time. It always held up when I was with Gable."

"Well, you and Zamir were just meant to be, and so are these babies." Neveah smiled, eyeing my stomach before turning her attention to Aurora.

She took Aurora's hand in hers. "And you." Ro, you and Anderson worked through your communication stuff, and things are better than ever between the two of you."

Aurora's lips sealed into a tight smile as she blinked back tears. "It was rocky for a little bit, but we made it through."

She pulled us into a sisterly group hug. "I love y'all forever," she said.

"We love you too," Aurora and I echoed.

Breaking the group embrace, Aurora asked, "Blou, do you have a sitter lined up for the twins?"

"We won't need anyone right away," I said. "Aunt Gina's going to come help out a few days a week."

"OK. When you do need someone, maybe you can consider Layla's sitter. She's looking for more work. Anderson and I love her."

"Wait. The one who doesn't accept electronic payments?" Neveah cut her eyes in Aurora's direction.

Aurora's eyes grew wide. "I meant to tell y'all about that," she said. "Apparently, her mom had been using her identity to scam people. Digital payment systems were one way she was doing it. Got her banned."

"What?" Neveah and I exclaimed in unison.

"That's why she could only accept cash?" I asked. "Wow."

"*Mm-hm*," Aurora hummed. "She didn't want to tell us at first. She thought we would judge her based on her mom's behavior, but once her mom was arrested for fraud, she confided in us. She's completely cut her mom off, so she needs the work."

"Dang, girl. That's messed up," Neveah said.

"Yep. She moved in with her dad. He's been helping her since she's still in college. I feel so sorry for her. She's such a sweet girl."

"I'll let you know when I need her," I said.

"Well," Neveah sighed. "We better get back so I can finish glamming up." A grin spread across her face.

Aurora and I grinned back.

"Let's get it then," Aurora chirped, excitement sparkling in her eyes.

We walked back to the house, sharing the details of what we would change into for the reception after the pictures were taken. When we entered through the back door, I paused, stopping in my tracks.

"What is he doing here?" I whispered to Neveah.

She frowned. "I don't know," she whispered back. "I don't think Lukas invited him. We made the guest list together."

I walked away from my friends and strolled toward Gable.

As he reached for the knob to open the front door to leave, I gently tapped him on his shoulder.

"Gable." I said, softly. "What are you doing here?"

He turned to face me. His eyes searched mine, like he was trying to gauge what I was feeling.

It had been nearly a year ago since I'd last seen him. Zamir and I were having dinner with our planner finalizing the details of our small backyard wedding.

As we left the restaurant, Gable and his colleagues were entering. Ironically, it was the same restaurant where we'd met years ago.

We'd stopped to exchange a quick hello. His eyes held the same sadness that night that they had the day I told him I wanted a divorce—the day after he'd come back.

"Blou, there you are," Zamir's voice eased me out of the past. He walked up from behind and stood next to me, placing an arm around my waist.

I glanced up at him and smiled before training my eyes back on Gable.

"Gable, thank you again for dropping Amir off. I know Esa and I normally arrange to meet for my scheduled time with him," Zamir said.

A smile inched onto Gable's face. "No problem, man. I'm just glad I had the opportunity to spend more time with him while she's out of town on business. He's been doing so well. I'm just happy his condition isn't as advanced as mine, and most likely never will be. When I did the trial study to help myself, I had no idea I was also helping my own son."

Zamir grinned. "Yeap. A whole year without needing any transfusions. We finally got answers to many of the questions we've had for so long, and because of the advanced medication, hopefully he'll never need another transfusion."

I raised a brow and turned to Zamir. "Amir's here?" I asked. Gable dropping Amir off was different, but I guess it was a good thing since Gable was now a part of Amir's life too.

"Yes. He's upstairs with your aunt and uncle, Brave, and Fallon. I passed Aurora on the way down. She said Anderson and Layla are on the way here. He'll have his pal to play with soon."

I nodded. "Ah, OK." I warmed inside at the thought of how much Layla loves Amir. "She'll be happy to see him."

I rested my eyes back on Gable. "I'm glad to see you doing well, Gable," I added, my smile unfeigned.

"Thank you, Blou," he said. "I feel good most days. I have to take medication for the rest of my life but thanks to the trial, I'm here." His eyes shifted to my stomach. "Congratulations to the both of you. Amir told me you were expecting but now I can clearly see that for myself." He smiled, but his eyes flickered with something I could barely catch, remorse—maybe.

"Yeah, man." Zamir grinned. "It won't be long now."

"Blou," Aurora called out.

I turned toward her voice. She was standing at the top of the stairs with a hand on her hip. "Girl, come on. We've got to get ready, and help Neveah too."

I turned back to Gable. "Well, it was nice seeing you."

"Same." He leaned in, and we exchanged a brief side hug.

I looked at Zamir. "OK, babe. Duty calls."

Zamir nodded in Gable's direction. "Thanks again. See you around, man."

Linking our fingers, we turned and strolled hand in hand toward the stairs.

Neveah and Lukas exchanged their vows on the beach, standing in front of a large arch decorated with flowers galore. The flowers matched the floral displays tied to each of the white chairs arranged for guests.

The reception was equally beautiful, held on the massive lower deck that extended out from the beach house, decorated with the same floral décor. The mid-May weather was a perfect mix for the light breeze drifting from the ocean.

The DJ was spinning old school music when Zamir pulled me onto the dance floor. He gently twirled me around as *"Brick House"* bellowed from the speakers.

We laughed as he pulled me into him. I linked my arms around his neck and gazed into his eyes.

"I love you so much, Blou Skies."

I frowned.

He tilted his head, his eyes squinting. "What?" he asked.

I stepped back and looked down to the floor. "My water just broke."

His eyes grew wide as he stared down at the small puddle pooling around my feet.

Four hours and forty-five minutes later, I watched Zamir as he sat on the couch in my hospital room, holding two adorable babies.

I was filled with joy as he glanced from one baby to the other making googly noises at them.

Brave left to take Aunt Gina and Uncle Lance home right after the babies were delivered, an hour ago. Aunt Gina said they'd had a long day and needed to rest their "old" bones. Brave promised he'd be coming back.

I slipped my mother's journal from under the pillow. Luckily, we had kept the bag in the car for the last week, just in case.

I must have read my mother's journal at least twenty times over the past two years. I opened it to the words that had stuck with me the most since the first day I read them: *My greatest prayer is that my children will love each other unconditionally and become one another's strongest supporters. That one day, they'll pass down the same values I hope to instill in them to their own children.*

Just to see what was in her heart and how much Brave and I both meant to her, even before our births, healed me in places I never knew could be mended.

Brave walked in with two balloons in one hand, one read *It's a Boy* and the other *It's a Girl* and a bouquet of white, yellow, and pink roses in the other.

I closed the journal and placed it on the table beside the bed. My eyes welled as he handed the roses to me.

"Brave, I—"

His eyebrows creased together. "I'm sorry, Blou. I didn't mean to—"

I waved my hand. "No. It's fine," I said, tears sliding down my cheeks. "I love the thought you put into this," I cried.

Zamir watched our exchange from across the room, scooting to the edge of the couch to stand. I gave him a reassuring smile that I was OK. He settled back into his seat with the babies.

"The white roses represent new beginnings, the pink ones to welcome our little Celest and our sweet boy, Elijah, and the yellow ones for the joy they bring," I explained. "Our mom wrote in her journal that when my dad found out she was pregnant with me, he gifted her a white rose and a pink rose."

"And she wrote, that he did the same when she was pregnant with me, except with a white and yellow rose," Brave added.

"She dried the roses and glued them to a page in her journal and wrote what each color represented." I smiled, holding up the journal.

"Ahh, OK," Zamir replied. "That's so cool."

"Yeap." Brave grinned. "It's even cooler that they are named after their grandparents, Cecily and Elias.

I took Brave's hand in mine and squeezed gently. Looking up at him, I whispered, "Thank you, baby bro."

"No. Thank you," he said.

"For what?" I asked.

"For grace." He winked.

What are your thoughts about Gable's choice to leave without saying anything to Blou? Should she have been included in the decision and given a choice to be by his side through the process?

Blou married Gable knowing she didn't want children, and he did. Was it selfish of her to accept his proposal?

Blou and Gable were still married when she had dinner with Zamir. Do you consider that cheating given the fact that she still had romantic feelings for Zamir?

Gable said that the baby he had with Esa was between him and Esa and had nothing to do with Blou. Could this be a valid point given the fact that Gable was not in Amir's life?

In your opinion, was Blou equally deceitful as Gable by hiding the abortion from both him and Zamir? Should Zamir have been included in the decision?

Should Aunt Gina have told Blou and Brave sooner about their mother choosing to have Brave, knowing that she was at risk? Do you think that if they had known sooner it would have helped their strained relationship?

Knowing that she had another child to raise, was it selfish of Cecily to have Brave knowing the risk? And should Elias have spoken up instead of leaving the decision solely to Cecily?

Do you think Aurora was right about Gable being controlled?

Zamir decided to stay in Amir's life even after finding out he isn't his biological child. Now that Gable is also in Amir's life, should Zamir have more say-so when it comes to decisions concerning Amir, than Gable has?

Since Zamir is Amir's father, that would make Blou his stepmother since she married him. If you were in Blou's shoes, would it be difficult for you to accept Amir as your stepson given, he is Gable's biological child?

Brave wanted so much to be accepted and valued by Blou, do you think that is why he jumped from one thing to the next looking for something fulfilling? Do you think Blou was too hard on him given that he was so young?

Neveah felt that Blou jumped into marriage too fast with Gable. Do you think there is a certain time frame it takes to really get to know someone? Do you think Blou really knew Gable before she married him?

Was Gabriella wrong for telling Gable about running into Blou and Zamir at the coffee shop given his condition?

Blou decided to have children with Zamir but not with Gable. Why do you think that is?

Acknowledgments

My first novel. Writing this book was so much fun. The ideas of this book played in my head for so long before they actually made it to paper. Without a good support system it is hard to make your dreams come true.

To my wonderful, patient, loving husband, thank you. You've listened to my ideas and brainstorming, stayed patient while I let things go to make time to write, did all the extra things necessary to keep our life running smoothing on top of the load you already carry. You are amazing and truly the person I need by my side as I accomplish all that my heart desires.

My lovely circle of friends. As I decided what Blou's circle of friends would be like, I thought of you all. The circle that gives freely, keeps it real and hold each other up when we find it challenging to stand on our own. Kisa, Tip, NaTesha, Rineta, Ashlyn, I love y'all so much. Y'all are the sisters I was able to choose.

My passion to write came when I was a young girl. Partly, because my mother nourished my love for reading by keeping the thick romance books coming. Which is probably why I am also a hopeless romantic (LOL). And my father, who led by example by showing his love for reading. My love for reading turned into a love for writing. Thank you mom and dad.

To my biological sisters, Carol and Angela, your love and support runs so far and deep. I am grateful for you.. Thank you so much.

Hugs and kisses to my brother, Chris. Man, to find a true friend in a brother is a blessing. Your support is just as strong as the love I feel every time I see you and you wrap me up in a hug. Thank you brother.

I'm certainly thankful for my bonus mother-in-love, Gloria. Your creative support is appreciated more than you know. Thank you for mentioning my books in your state.

My mother-in-law, Marian, it feels wonderful to see my books displayed in your living room when I step in your home. Thank you.

Kiaria, Kelvin, Daneisha, Tyrek, Cam, Jaiune, Kasie, Zarah and Yanis, I'm blessed to have you all as my children and grandchildren. So much of my motivation to accomplish the things that I have came from my desire to inspire you all.

Last but certainly not lest, I thank God who has never wavered, never failed me and has always blessed me above all that I have asked.

ABOUT THE AUTHOR

April is a marriage and family therapist, a devoted wife, and a proud mother whose love for storytelling began in childhood. Her deep understanding of emotional healing and family dynamics shapes both her clinical work and her writing, which spans genres and generations.

She is the author of an award-winning faith-based devotional journal, four children's books, and a candid memoir that explores resilience, grace, and the journey toward healing. On the Edge of Grace marks her debut in adult fiction, offering a tender, layered story about forgiveness, family, and the quiet strength it takes to begin again.

Connect with April
IG: Instagram.com/Iamaprilyolan
www.aprilyjonestherapy.com
Blog: www.justbeingthejones.com/biwaj

<u>Also By April Y. Jones</u>

Grow On: A Spiritual and Mental Wellness Devotional Journal

Blended Family Series:
My Bonus Mommy
When Gigi Visits
Kiaria's Birthday Surprise

If It Makes You Happy

Set Me Free: A Journey Toward Self-Freedom
A Memoir

www.ingramcontent.com/pod-product-compliance
Lightning Source LLC
Chambersburg PA
CBHW031958180726
48283CB00008B/2488